The Ghost
of Ballyhooly

By the Same Author

ACCENT ON APRIL
ALMOST LIKE SISTERS
ANGEL ON SKIS
THE BOY NEXT DOOR
A BREATH OF FRESH AIR
THE COUNTRY COUSIN
FANCY FREE
JENNY KIMURA
MYSTERY AT LOVE'S CREEK
MYSTERY IN MARRAKECH
MYSTERY ON SAFARI
PASSPORT TO ROMANCE
THE SCARLET SAIL
SPICE ISLAND MYSTERY
STARS IN HER EYES
A TIME FOR TENDERNESS
PUBLISHED BY WILLIAM MORROW AND COMPANY

THE BLACK SPANIEL MYSTERY
A GIRL CAN DREAM
GOING ON SIXTEEN
LASSO YOUR HEART
LOVE, LAURIE
PAINTBOX SUMMER
PUPPY STAKES
6 ON EASY STREET
SPRING COMES RIDING
SPURS FOR SUZANNA
A TOUCH OF MAGIC
TWO'S COMPANY
PUBLISHED BY THE WESTMINSTER PRESS

The Ghost of Ballyhooly

BETTY CAVANNA

William Morrow & Company | New York

Author's Note

The setting of this book is real. Ballyhooly Castle exists, near the village of Ballyhooly in County Cork, Ireland. I have stayed there with my family over the Christmas holidays. However, the characters in the mystery are fictional and the incidents imaginary. For the purposes of my story, I have advanced the opening of the salmon season on the Blackwater River by one month.

The Ghost
of Ballyhooly

1

Christmas in a castle—an Irish castle! The prospect seemed to Kristy too romantic to be real. Yet she knew, after a term in a Dublin school, that Ireland was full of castles, many of them crumbling into ruin, but others still occupied, although few were still intact.

"We're taking Ballyhooly Castle on the Blackwater River for the holidays," her grandfather had written from the United States. "Since most of our children and grandchildren seem to be living abroad this year, we thought it would be fun to bring Christmas to you instead of wishing hopelessly that you could come to us."

"You mean Grandpa's renting the whole palace," young Sam asked in a breathless whisper, "just for us?"

His father chuckled, and rumpled the child's hair affectionately. "It's a castle, Sambo, not a palace. More like a

11

big house hitched onto an old tower. And we'll need a big house, for nine of us."

"Nine?" Kristy began ticking off people on her fingers. "Uncle Robert and Aunt Irene, Grandpa and Grandma, you and Mommy, Sam and me."

"Don't forget Ned," her mother reminded her, turning from the pile of clean laundry she was sorting. "Ned's almost three. He's a person in his own right."

"He's just a baby," Sam snorted with disgust. "He doesn't count."

Kristy caught a glimpse of her reflection in a window-pane and automatically raised a hand to adjust the fall of her long brown hair, which hung straight and thick to her shoulders. Sam caught the gesture, interpreted it quickly, muttered, "Oh, stop admiring yourself," and then slumped into a chair. "Nobody's ever my age," he complained, and added wistfully, "If only Ned were eleven or twelve, or even ten."

"Well, he isn't," said Kristy with perverse satisfaction. Her green eyes regarded her younger brother balefully and she marveled that there had been a time in her life when she had regarded him as companionable and even rather endearing. Lately, Sam seemed bent on irritating her.

Holding out a stack of towels and facecloths, her mother tactfully took steps to prevent a dispute. "Carry these to the linen closet, will you, dear?" she said to

12

Kristy, who accepted them dreamily and walked off into the hall, which connected the bedrooms with the rest of the sprawling flat. Absently, she walked straight past the closet and carried the towels back to her own room, where she balanced them on a windowsill, anchoring the stack with her chin. She stood for several minutes staring out over the university campus in the direction of the city, where smoke clouds blended with a cold December mist.

Oregon, she was thinking, could be in another world. Her former school friends, Linda and Beth, Ginny Carter, and the rest of the girls she had known well at one time, seemed to recede into the distant past. Dublin, on the other hand, was as familiar as the town of Eugene had once been. She had mastered the intricate bus system, learned to find her way through back streets like a native, and could tell at a glance the value of a sweater (pullovers, they were called here) made in the Aran Islands. But an Irish castle—that would be something altogether different! She tried to imagine how it would look, but failed utterly. The only castle she had actually visited was the one where she had hung by her toes trying to kiss the Blarney stone while her mother stood by nervously, murmuring, "Darling, think of the germs!"

From Kristy's present perspective, that day, too, seemed long ago, associated with the panic and excitement of being transplanted to Ireland. She had felt anxious about everything in September, especially the necessity of making new friends in a strange school and the problem of understanding the teachers, who sometimes sounded as though they were speaking a foreign language, so different was their pronunciation from hers.

Now such fears seemed hysterical. She could look at things—and people—more constructively and less emotionally than she had been able to in those early days in Dublin. No longer was she swept by waves of homesickness, nor did she pray for the post to contain a letter from Jeff Reynolds. His promises to write once a week had proved overambitious. What was there, after all, to say?

Her world had changed in these past months during which she had reached the reasonably attractive age of sixteen. Jeff's, presumably, had remained the same. Undoubtedly he still came and went along the school corridors with that loose, easy stride. His fair hair still straggled on his neck, and his brown eyes were still compelling. "Jeff." His name, repeated in a whisper, no longer made her tingle. Instead, there leaped to her mind the name of a lad with tousled, curly hair and laughing eyes, who could whistle an Irish tune as though he were schooled for the stage and make an American girl feel like a princess about to step from a golden coach.

"Michael." It was a softer name altogether than Jeff. Michael's brogue was like a feather's touch, it was so beguiling. She wondered what he would say when she told him about the castle. Ballyhooly on the Blackwater River.

*   *   *

"Sure, of course I know where it is!" Michael replied
at once when Kristy and he met after school the next day.
"In County Cork, not more than four miles from Fermoy,
where my Aunt Sheila lives. A great spot for fishing, that
section of the Blackwater used to be. Always wanted to
try my luck when I went visiting, but of course it wasn't
permitted."

"Not allowed? Why not?" Kristy asked curiously.
"Isn't the river free?"

"Not for the likes of us," Michael told her. "All the
good stretches of water along the rivers of Ireland belong
to the big landowners. You start fishing in the Duke of
Devonshire's waters and they'll pop you in prison faster
than you can say Jack Robinson."

"How very curious," Kristy murmured, thinking of the
rushing trout streams of Oregon, of the rivers and lakes
to which Sam and her father drove on Saturday excursions. "If we're living on a river Dad's going to want to
go fishing," she said, half to herself.

"Oh, he'll be O.K.," Michael assured her. "If you rent
a castle in those parts the fishing rights go along with it.
As a matter of fact that's the only reason most foreigners
lease a place on a river, so they can fish."

"What do you catch in the Blackwater? Trout?
Perch?"

Michael threw back his head and whooped with laugh-

15

ter. "Not likely! It's a salmon river, Kristy, one of the great ones. Or it used to be."

"Used to be. What do you mean?" Kristy asked, with a curiosity that was as characteristic as her tendency to daydream. Michael's reply was forestalled by the arrival of the bus that Kristy must take back to the campus of Trinity College, where her family lived in a flat reserved for visiting professors. She waved a quick good-bye and swung aboard, while Michael stood on the curb looking slightly bereft. From behind the cloudy window Kristy waved again. I actually think he'll miss me, she mused, not without a mild feeling of satisfaction. It was nice to be admired.

Michael is so very Irish, she thought as she sat clutching her books and rocking with the motion of the bus. With his high coloring and his blue eyes and his quick changes of mood he's as much a part of this country as the perpetual mist. Kristy had learned a great deal about the Irish in four months; she had learned that they were friendly, sentimental, convivial, often sad, and frequently poor, but never downcast. The men loved to gather in pubs and drink stout, a dark, alcoholic beverage slightly stronger than beer. It looked like thick Coca-Cola with whipped cream on top and tasted bitter and rather unpleasant. "Just as well," her father had said when Kristy had taken a swallow from his glass and shuddered with distaste. "Just as well."

Stephen Henderson, who was apt to repeat himself absentmindedly when he was talking to one of his children, was a mathematician, an abstract algebraist, who had come to Trinity College on sabbatical leave from the University of Oregon, where he customarily taught. He was a tall, shaggy-haired man who enjoyed tennis and fishing but eschewed golf, one of Ireland's popular sports. His most satisfying hours were spent with a pencil and paper working out intricate, abstruse problems that had never before been solved.

Kristy knew that her father was highly respected in his field, and that many people considered him a genius, but she hadn't a clue as to what his specialty really involved. Her interests lay in the humanities. She loved to read, attempted from time to time to write verse, and toyed with the idea of majoring in journalism in college, because the assignments of a foreign correspondent sounded so adventurous.

"There's no telling what Kristy will do with her life," she had heard her mother say recently to an inquiring friend. "She's still at the formative stage."

Kristy supposed this was true, but she felt a great deal more grown-up than she had four months ago. Sam's teasing notwithstanding, she was no longer interested primarily in herself. She had become aware of the problems in the world around her, and she was apt to join her Irish companions in discussions of politics and national

17

ideologies, of war and of conservation, employing words that had been meaningless to her until very recently.

These boys and girls with whom she talked were restless and deeply committed to the ideas they considered right. Most of them were anxious to get away from the restrictions of home, yet few would have the opportunity of going to college, which Kristy took for granted.

Michael was one of the lucky ones. He got top grades in the sixth form, a year ahead of Kristy's class, and he would probably get a scholarship to the university. He had admitted one day that he dreamed of going to the United States to graduate school, then laughed at himself for the notion. "The Irish are the most imaginative people in the world," he added boastfully, "but these days they seldom manage to get far from the counties they were born in."

When she listened to such a remark Kristy felt very American indeed. There was an air of resignation about the statement that made her impatient and rebellious. "You can break the pattern if you try hard enough," she had said encouragingly. She was remembering this conversation as the bus ground to a halt at the edge of the campus and she gathered her books to her chest and followed the other commuters down the steps to the street. There were some things about the Irish she would never understand, and one was the acceptance of a destiny they apparently considered inevitable.

At the flat her mother was airing suitcases for the

fortnight's sojourn at Ballyhooly. "We must take lots of woolens," she said from the bedroom doorway. "Even in the south it's apt to be very cold."

"But I thought there were palm trees and things in County Cork," Kristy objected. "I thought we were going to be *warm* for once."

Valerie Henderson sat back on her heels and shook the hair out of her eyes. "I'm afraid that's wishful thinking, Kristy dear. In any event, I'm counting on a cold and drafty barn of a place, and I advise you to take along your ski underwear and sweaters and slacks. I've never yet heard of anyone being warm in an Irish country house."

"Castle," corrected Kristy. "I wish we knew more about it. Ballyhooly, I mean."

"So do I," said her mother, as she considered the relative merits of a pair of gray flannel slacks and a brown tweed skirt.

"If only Grandpa had sent us a snapshot."

"I doubt if he has one."

"Maybe there's something about Ballyhooly in the library," Kristy suggested with a flash of inspiration. "I think I'll go have a look."

The university library was a busy place in the late afternoon, crowded with students doing research for papers or working on special assignments. Although Kristy carried a card granting her permission to use the books, she felt conspicuous as she waited her turn at the files in

19

the reference room, because obviously she was too young to be a college student. Once she had pulled out the drawer labeled B, however, she forgot her surroundings and became absorbed. Ballys were there by the score— Ballyadam, Ballyadeen, Ballyduff, Ballygrillihan, Ballygyroe. Finally Kristy's finger, turning the cards, stopped.

"Ballyhooly," she read. "Baile Atha hUlla." This must be the old Gaelic name, she decided logically. There was a subtitle reference to a book on Irish history, then another subtitle reading "Castle," and a reference to a volume entitled *Residences of Lord Roche.* Kristy wrote down the numbers that would locate the books in the stacks, but it was the final reference which really captured her interest: "See also *Ghosts in Irish Castles,* 712-413 C."

She took the slip of paper containing her requests to the librarian at the desk and handed it to her with a sense of anticipation, wondering especially about the ghost bit. Wouldn't Sam be delighted if Ballyhooly Castle came complete with midnight visitors!

Waiting with simulated patience for the books to be brought from the stacks, she let her eyes roam over the room, resting on the faces of students bent over their books. At first all the Irish had looked alike to her, red-cheeked and chunky, but now she recognized as many types as she would have been able to distinguish in any such group in the United States. Likeable faces, she thought, whether homely or beautiful. Nice people, no longer strangers, good natured and—

"Here you are, miss."

"Oh, thank you," said Kristy, turning.

"I'm afraid we can't find the third number, but we'll look again."

Kristy tried to conceal her disappointment, because the book on ghosts interested her most of all. "If you would, please!" she begged, and with the other two books went to the nearest vacant chair.

There was a musty smell to the volumes she opened on the table before her. Obviously, from the way the bindings cracked, they were seldom used. The history book was ponderous and its author had been unconcerned with so small a village as Ballyhooly. Kristy learned that BaileAtha hUlla could be translated as the Town-of-the-Ford-of-the-Apples, and that eight small caves nearby had yielded remains of mammoth, reindeer, and Irish elk. Also in the vicinity, two miles northwest, was an old dolmen, or burial mound, called Labbacallee—the Hag's Bed—where five bodies had been discovered. Since there was no mention of when or of whom, Kristy didn't find this item especially worthy of note.

The second book was slightly more informative. A Roche castle in Ballyhooly had been wrecked in one of the many rebellions of the 1600's by Cromwell's troops and lay in partial ruin until it was restored in 1862 by a certain

21

Lady Listowell, after which it became known as Ballyhooly Castle. "Situated on the banks of the Blackwater River beyond the village of this name, it is surrounded by a terraced garden and faces on broad meadows going down to the river. In the park is a private chapel, and on the river bank a boathouse of recent construction," read Kristy. "The river is not only famous for its salmon but is most picturesque."

She closed the book with the feeling that the castle was likely to be more intriguing than even Sam anticipated. Any building that dated back to the seventeenth century and had survived Cromwell's crushing victory over the Irish Catholics was bound to be romantic.

And if there were a ghost to boot!

Kristy returned the two books to the desk and asked the librarian if she had been able to locate the other volume.

"What was the title again?"

"Ghosts in Irish Castles," Kristy replied.

"I'm afraid it's been misplaced on the shelves," the woman said. "We'll have to make a thorough search. Could you come back tomorrow?"

"I suppose so," Kristy agreed reluctantly.

With a hint of a smile, the librarian asked, "Is it very important?"

"It may be," answered Kristy. "To be quite honest, I can't really tell."

* * *

One thing was certain. The missing book whetted Kristy's curiosity, and she hurried to the library the next afternoon direct from school, only to be disappointed once more. "I'm afraid, dear," the same librarian explained, "that we can't find it anywhere. There's no record to show it has been taken out, at least not properly. It's scarcely a book an undergraduate would need for his studies, unless of course he was doing a paper on national folklore. Anyway," she added with a sigh, "it seems to have disappeared."

"That's too bad. Will you let me know if it turns up?" Kristy left her name and address, and walked back to the flat feeling frustrated. That night at dinner she told her family about her investigations. "I almost found you a ghost," she said ruefully to Sam, who had listened to her discoveries without much interest.

"What do you mean, a ghost?" asked her brother warily.

"There might be a ghost at Ballyhooly. Wouldn't you like that?"

"Are you kidding?" In spite of himself, Sam's eyes began to sparkle.

"Sort of," Kristy confessed. "Maybe there was a ghost, once upon a time, but he seems to have disappeared. And maybe he never existed, even in the pages of a book."

2

"Ballyhooly. What a marvelous name!" murmured Kristy's mother. She sat with a map of Ireland spread out on her knees in the front seat of a European Ford rented for the drive across the island.

Stephen Henderson nodded. "At once amusing, improbable, and whimsical. In other words, typically Irish."

In the back seat Sam squirmed, stiff from the long ride, and Kristy yawned plaintively. "Is it much farther?"

Her father didn't answer. Instead he repeated a favorite quotation: " 'We are the music makers, And we are the dreamers of dreams.' " Half turning, but without taking his eyes from the next curve of the narrow, hedge-bordered road, he added, "An Irishman said that, a poet named O'Shaughnessy. Do you know the rest, Kristy?"

Kristy mumbled a negative. She was bored and didn't

24

care how the poem proceeded. Sam was an itch, always getting his ankles entangled with hers. The car was too cramped for comfort, the hours of driving too long, the roads too twisting for speed. Even the lure of Ballyhooly Castle was no longer tempting. Only the prospect of seeing her grandparents sustained her.

She loved them in a completely different way from that in which she loved her mother and father. Since they lived on the East Coast she saw them infrequently, but she always felt at home with them at once. Her grand-mother, a small, well-made woman, born in Mississippi, still had a slight Southern accent, along with the gracious manners acquired in her childhood. Kristy's grandmother came straight from Mary Washington College to work for a publishing firm in Boston, and there she met a young Harvard professor and married him within six months. The time was the late twenties and the first World War was a decade past, the depression still to come. Forty years later Christine Henderson, for whom Kristy had been named, occasionally reviewed books for a Boston newspa-per and contributed pieces to magazines. Her husband, retired from teaching, continued to maintain a laboratory at the university. As grandparents the Hendersons could be loving and friendly without the irksome discipline par-ents were forced to dispense. No wonder Kristy was fond of them!

Her Uncle Robert and Aunt Irene she knew only

slightly. Their son Ned had been born in Philadelphia, then moved with them to Paris, where they had been living for the past year. Irene was a painter—rather a good one, Kristy's mother said of her young sister-in-law. Robert was studying for an advanced degree on a fellowship at the Sorbonne, and Kristy had been told that he was an Orientalist, but wasn't at all sure what that meant.

"Do you suppose Ned speaks French?" Sam asked unexpectedly.

"At the age of three he probably doesn't speak much of anything," Kristy muttered grumpily.

"Don't be too sure," said their mother from the front seat. "At two and a half you were chattering away a mile a minute."

"I thought boys were usually late talkers," Kristy murmured tenaciously.

"Not necessarily," her mother replied as she bent her head to study the road map. "Knockmealdown Mountains. Knock-me-all-down. Isn't that wonderful!"

"You've got to be kidding," said Sam, and inched forward to look at the map over his mother's shoulder. Then Kristy cried suddenly, "Look, a river! Could it be the Blackwater? Maybe we're almost there!"

"I think it is the Blackwater, but we follow it for several miles—" Mrs. Henderson broke off and started tracing the route with her finger. "Now I'm beginning to get excited."

26

The lilt in her mother's voice made Kristy straighten up and appraise the passing countryside with a new sense of anticipation, as the clouds parted and a wavering sun glinted on the wet road. Sheep grazed in meadows glimpsed through screens of trees along the river, which was broad, flat, and as black as its name. The stream appeared and disappeared at intervals as the road curved past an occasional cluster of cottages and country houses roofed with shining slate. Eventually it passed under a bridge in a village called Ballyduff and after a few miles widened at a good-sized market town named Fermoy.

"Six more kilometers!" murmured the driver in a tone of relief.

Kristy got a comb out of her shoulder bag and began to work away at the tangles in her hair, while her brother regarded her with patent disapproval. "Always primping."

"Be quiet, Sam. And stop arguing, the two of you," ordered Mr. Henderson, coping with the probability in advance. He slowed down as the traffic thickened, then made an abrupt left turn at the principal intersection, where the main road from Dublin turned south. Again the river appeared, tumbling over low falls to a broad sweep of water rushing away downstream. A half-timbered hotel crouched by a bridge, and a road sign, pointing left, read: *Ballyhooly, Castletownroche, Mallow.*

"At last!" said Kristy's mother. "It's the first sign to Ballyhooly we've seen."

Fifteen minutes later the Hendersons came to a dead end on a treeless village street of close-packed, gray houses hugging a narrow sidewalk. Not a pedestrian was in sight, although a corner pub had its door ajar, as though expecting customers. To the right the spire of a church rose against the sky, and to the left the road curved downhill. Sam craned forward, then suddenly yelled, "Look! maybe that's the castle!" He had spotted a crenellated tower rising from a stand of trees.

"I bet you're right," his father said, and a minute later turned into a crushed-stone drive leading past a square cottage and through a wrought iron gate into a small park. Leafless apple trees, carefully pruned, lined the drive, and ahead lay a paved courtyard faced on one side by the castle tower and on the other by stables and a greenhouse. Matted ivy clung to the tower walls, and at its base a few hardy geraniums flaunted bright red flowers in defiance of imminent frosty death.

Kristy, the first out of the car, looked up at the tower in frank delight. So Ballyhooly was a real castle after all! A huge black raven wheeled in the gray sky and the stones beneath her feet were wet and cold, but although the sun had disappeared again the weather could no longer dampen her spirits. She raised her arms and stretched, lifting the hair from the back of her neck and shivering in anticipation. "Isn't this going to be fun!"

"How do we get in?" Sam was twisting a forelock of straight blond hair and looking at the huge oak door, brass-studded and barred, sent into the weathered wall.

His father laughed. "Around the corner, I expect. This is the tower, son, not the house."

As he spoke, a slight, stringy man in work clothes emerged from one of the stables. He carried a spade, which he propped against the side of the building as soon as he caught sight of the car. Without hurrying, he came across the courtyard and approached Kristy's father. "You Mr. Henderson?" he asked rather listlessly.

"That's right."

"I was expectin' somebody older," the man said, while Kristy stood by thinking that she had seldom seen a more expressionless face. The eyes, steely-gray like the sky, were small and close-set, the mouth was thin-lipped, the cheeks lined and sunken. He stood quite motionless as he regarded the tall American.

Kristy's father grinned. "I'm the younger Henderson —Stephen," he explained. "It's my father who rented the place." This explanation, although it seemed acceptable, did not change the man's expression. "My name's O'Malley," he said. "Fergus O'Malley. I'm the gardener here."

"Glad to meet you, Fergus. This is Mrs. Henderson and these are our children, Christine and Sam. At least Sam *was* here, a second ago."

29

Kristy and her mother smiled and greeted the gardener pleasantly. Fergus responded with a jerk of his scrawny neck. "You want help with the bags?" he asked.

"That would be nice," said Mrs. Henderson, while her husband started to unstrap the luggage racked on the car roof.

At this point Sam reappeared around the corner of the tower at a gallop. "I found out how you get in," he shouted. "There are two women in blue coats. One's Nora and the other's Mary." Grabbing his mother's hand, he urged her, "Come see."

"First I want you to meet Mr. O'Malley. Fergus, this is our son, Sam."

The boy and man, equally taciturn, grunted in acknowledgment of the introduction. "Here, Sam," said his father, handing down a long canvas case. "You can carry my fishing rods."

Fergus made a sound that was either a snort or a cough. "Salmon season don't open till the first of the year," he muttered.

"I know. But we'll be here until the fourth," said Mr. Henderson, "and that will give me three good days."

"Not many fish around anyways, not this winter." Fergus seemed bound to be pessimistic. He shook his head dolefully as he picked up three heavy suitcases and carried them around the corner of the tower.

Kristy and her mother followed the gardener and Sam,

30

who was leading the procession like a majordomo, the canvas rod case his baton. In the doorway of the main house, approached by a broad ramp and hitched to the castle tower by a connecting wing, waited two rosy-cheeked young women with immaculate bright blue smocks belted over warm woolen dresses. One was plump and smiling, the other slender and serious-faced, as became her position of authority. "I'm Nora," she said. "I take care of the castle year round. This is Mary, who comes to help when we have guests."

Before Mrs. Henderson could reply, a series of short staccato honks came from the direction of the park, and immediately the scene changed to one of happy confusion. The elder Hendersons had arrived in another car, picked up that morning at Shannon Airport, and suddenly everybody was running back and forth, hailing and hugging one another, while Nora and Mary took the suitcases from Fergus at the door and carried them into a broad hall.

"Kristy!" her grandmother cried, looking slim and elegant in a gray tweed coat that matched her short, breeze-tossed hair. "You're taller than I am." After kissing her lightly on the cheek, she held Kristy off by the shoulders. "You're a young lady! And you've grown so pretty. Oh, my dear, it's lovely to see you again."

Her greeting to Sam was just as affectionate. The occasion soon became a happy family house party, with everyone trooping around exploring the castle and allowing Nora and Mary to assign them the bedrooms they considered appropriate.

The grandparents and Kristy's mother and father were given big, comfortable rooms across the hall from one another. Furnished almost identically, there were wardrobes instead of closets, twin beds with down puffs, handsome antique writing desks, and chintz-curtained bay windows that looked out over a steeply terraced garden to green meadows on the river's edge.

Beyond a French door at the end of the central hall lay a small balcony, where the view made Kristy catch her breath in delight. On the left the river curved to a stone bridge reflected in the still water, and on the right it broadened to a reach visible for a mile or more. From the opposite shore rose the Nagles Mountains, purple hills flowing into one another, tier on tier, below the racing clouds. The scene was beautiful but astonishingly empty. No smoke rose from cottage chimneys. Not a house could be glimpsed on the wooded slopes. Mauve, indigo, black, and silver, the colors melted and joined in smooth concealment of any pattern of life.

"Hey, Kristy! Come look at your room. It's right next to mine."

"Naturally!" Kristy spoke in mock despair as she followed her brother back to an ell that faced the tower courtyard. The river was out of sight; only a stretch of rock garden could be seen from a window looking east. Beyond the garden a copse concealed the road as it dipped to the bridge, and among the dark trees Kristy could discern whitish, rectangular shapes which she recognized, after a moment or two, as gravestones. It seemed rather eerie to have a burial ground so close.

She was luckier than Sam, however, who had no view whatever, except of the tower. Nevertheless, this seemed to suit him perfectly. He stood gazing up at its crenellated top in fascination. "Golly," he murmured, "wait till I tell the kids at home about this!"

The heart of the house was the living room, or drawing room, as Nora called it. Furnished with comfortable overstuffed chairs and sofas, bookcases, antique Irish tables of faded mahogany, and warmed by a peat fire burning on an open hearth, it was the place where the entire family gathered for tea. In the midst of this ceremony the Russells arrived, having thriftily taken a student flight from Paris to Dublin, a train from Dublin to Mallow, and a bus to Ballyhooly, lugging their three-year-old son and their heavy suitcases to the castle on foot.

Ned, a chubby, brown-eyed child, proved as articulate as Kristy's mother had predicted. He spoke English in fairly complete sentences, interspersed with an occasional French phrase. Far from being shy, he was vociferous in his delight over Sam, whom he appropriated at once as a playmate. Kristy he considered warily, as though the world he was building for himself need not necessarily contain girls.

Surprisingly, Kristy found that she was rather hurt by this attitude, and was at some pains to capture Ned's attention. "Isn't he darling!" she said to her aunt, with a stirring of the maternal impulse she had long ago felt for a favorite doll.

Ned responded by staring at her soberly out of round, dark eyes. "Darling," he repeated, but turned and jabbed a pudgy finger at Sam. The adults all laughed, but Sam blushed furiously. "You can't say that, Ned," he objected. "I'm a boy."

From teatime until dinner was served at seven o'clock there was constant going and coming from the drawing room. People were unpacking, and Sam was racing in and out, reporting each new discovery. "The kitchen's down below the dining room and there's a dumbwaiter big enough to ride in, if you curl up in a ball," he said at one point. At another he told Kristy, "I found the chapel. It's behind another gate and there are some people from the village fixing it up for Christmas with holly and stuff." He leaned against her chair. "You ought to come see."

Kristy shook her head. She was quite happy here with the grown-ups, listening to the conversation of relatives who had not seen one another for a year or more. She remembered Aunt Irene as a gentle, large-boned young woman with soft, curling hair pinned on top of her head in a casual knot, but she had forgotten her sense of humor and the directness of her glance from eyes the clear, light color of amber held to the sun.

Twelve years younger than Kristy's father, Irene Henderson had met Robert Russell while she was studying painting at the Beaux Arts in Paris, and they had married before he started working on his master's degree at the University of Pennsylvania. Each had a penchant for France, and no one in the family was surprised when the couple elected to return, Robert to study Chinese and Oriental religions at the Sorbonne, while Irene found a nursery school for Ned and went back to painting in a studio at the Beaux Arts.

Kristy found her Uncle Robert more difficult to understand than her young and artistic aunt. Although he was nearly the same age as his wife, Robert's bushy hair and heavy beard made him look several years her senior. Like his brother-in-law, he was tall and thin. He had gray eyes that crinkled at the corners and an unexpected teasing approach to people, which might, Kristy suspected, conceal a social diffidence engendered by the Henderson clan. With Ned he was charming and playful, but with Kristy and her family he seemed vaguely ill at ease. Although he made repeated efforts to be witty he seemed to fall short of the mark. Perhaps he'd relax, Kristy decided, when he got to know them all better. In the meantime she found Aunt Irene more comfortable to be with than her uncle.

Kristy watched her take care of Ned, standing by as he had his evening bath and supper before being put to bed. The child was overexcited, and the strangeness of his room elicited a few strident wails of protest, but he soon settled down and went to sleep.

Going back to the drawing room, Kristy investigated the bookshelves, riffling through a leather-bound volume entitled *Fishing Rivers of Ireland,* running a finger along a row of musty Victorian novels, and filing away in her memory the names of two paperback mysteries that might be entertaining to read on a rainy day.

Sam had discovered a chess set and was setting it up on a small table. "Come on, play a game with me," he urged his sister.

"You know I hate chess. Ask Dad."

"He always says, 'Later on.' "

Kristy capitulated, but her heart wasn't in the contest. The pawns seemed to move about the board with an impetus of their own, and her queen was soon captured. Outside the windows the silvered river had disappeared in the quick fall of night. A wind had risen, and a tree branch scratched against a pane, while an owl hooted in the distance. Nora came in to close the curtains and poke up the fire. "Please, Miss Kristy, tell your grandmother I'll ring a bell when dinner is ready," she said.

Kristy glanced up from the game. "Thank you, Nora. I'll be glad to."

"Your turn," Sam prodded, knowing that his opponent would be mated in two moves.

Kristy yawned, and to her brother's satisfaction made the obvious move. As he was chortling over the ease with which he had won the game, the adults, who had changed for dinner, straggled back into the room. Uncle Robert arrived last, closing the door to shut out the cold draft from the hall. He was carrying a volume of Irish verse found in his bedroom. "There's another book *you* might like," he said to Sam. "It's called *Ghosts in Irish Castles,* and it's on the third shelf."

Sam looked only mildy interested, but Kristy was on her feet in a flash. "I know about that book!" she cried. "It has something in it on Ballyhooly. Can I go get it, please?"

The main hall, with ten-foot-high ceilings, was lit dimly with a single fixture, and the doors on either side were always kept closed. The Russells had rooms on the floor above, and Kristy took the stairs two at a time. She burst into the nursery by mistake, then closed the door softly and went on to the next room which, like her parents', looked out over the river.

Aunt Irene had turned off all the lights, so Kristy fumbled for a switch by the door, but apparently the lamps were controlled individually. In the dark she felt her way

37

toward the nearest piece of furniture, then stopped abruptly. The curtains had not been drawn, and outside, quite close to the house, a light was playing over the shubbery. It was small but bright, like a pencil flashlight, and its course seemed to lead downhill toward the fenced pasture by the river. Kristy stood and watched the moving beam for several minutes, not exactly fearful, but uneasy. Could some village boys be lurking about, peering in windows at the American strangers? Or could a thief be prowling on the property? The night had turned really cold, and the moon was hidden behind heavy, low-lying clouds. Certainly the evening wasn't inviting for an innocent stroll in the park of a privately-owned castle.

She shivered. As though on signal the light was extinguished and the window panes became blank once more. Quickly feeling her way along the edge of a bed to a night table, she located an old-fashioned switch attached to a dangling lamp cord. Suddenly the room was bright and cheerful, but before looking for the book Kristy went over and drew the curtains. She didn't want to be stared at like a fish in a clear glass bowl.

A few minutes later, back in the drawing room, she wondered whether she should mention the incident, but decided against it. Everyone looked so contented and cozy that she hadn't the heart to bring up a topic even mildly unpleasant. Instead she sank down on the sofa beside her mother and propped *Ghosts in Irish Castles* on her knees.

The book was slender but oversized, with a ragged dust jacket and a green binding spotted with mildew. The Table of Contents was brief and contained such intriguing chapter titles as "The Bloody Stones of Bourne" and "The Armless Rider of Castle Coolea." Near the bottom of the page Kristy's eye stopped. "Ballyhooly's Ghostly Catch. . . . 159."

"Here it is," she said to no one in particular, and quickly turned to page 159. Then she glanced at her mother in disappointment. "Oh, pooh!" she complained. "The whole bit about Ballyhooly is missing. See, the pages have been torn out. All of them!"

3

The morning of the twenty-third of December was unexpectedly sunny. Breakfast arrived in the dining room by dumbwaiter as soon as it was daylight, which wasn't until nine o'clock, Irish time. Right afterward Kristy and Sam set off to explore the village.

Ballyhooly, they quickly learned, was far from extensive. It consisted of a single street about the length of two city blocks, with squat row houses lining either side, which ended at a right-angled turn in the road that led to Mallow. Tucked between two of the houses was a general store with a single gas pump in front, and on the opposite side of the street, in the front room of one of the cramped little houses, was Ballyhooly's diminutive post office. Strategically situated on three of the four corners in the center of town were three pubs, all advertising Guinness stout.

Kristy, who had remembered to bring some money, bought colored postcards of the castle at Sullivan's, the general store, then went across the street to get some air mail stamps, with Sam tagging along beside her.

The postmistress, a spare, thin-haired woman with the air of an aging spinster, peered across the high counter at Kristy with unconcealed curiosity, which was satisfied the moment she heard her American accent. "Oh, you must be one of the Yanks at the castle," she said, then smiled in Sam's direction. "How are you getting along?"

"Just fine," Kristy replied, adding, "We only came yesterday."

The postmistress nodded. "Ring me up if you need anything. My name's Bessie Donovan and Ballyhooly 1 is the number. At the castle you're Ballyhooly 2. Nothing hard to remember about that."

Sam tugged at Kristy's sleeve. "Ask her if she knows where we can buy a Christmas tree."

Miss Donovan looked doubtful. "Better ask Fergus if he can find you one," she suggested. "Except in the towns, most people make do with holly. Still, he may know of someone cutting evergreens on his place."

Kristy thanked her, pocketed the change from a pound note, and went out to the street once more. Aside from a truck rumbling around the turn to Fermoy and a black-shawled woman with a market basket going into the grocery, there wasn't a living thing in sight. Nor was there a single tree to break the monotony of the facing rows of

41

secretive gray houses. Only in the distance, beyond the church at one end of the stark little village and the castle at the other, could she catch a glimpse of green.

"Well, that's that," she said to Sam. "Not a very lively place."

"Maybe it's too early in the morning for people to be around."

"It's past ten o'clock," Kristy said, "even if it does look like six-thirty back home."

Sam sighed. "Well, let's go ask Fergus about a Christmas tree."

"We'd better speak to Dad first," Kristy suggested sensibly as they left the main road and turned into the park. Here, at least, there was some activity. A plump, pink-faced woman in a red sweater was hanging out washing on a line at the side of the cottage, and from the front window of the neat little house five small faces peered eagerly. The children, Kristy reckoned, must have ranged from three to nine. Their cheeks were as rosy as apples, their eyes large with curiosity. However, when she waved and called "Hello" they retreated into the shadows, shy as gazelles.

Their mother was less inhibited. "Good morning!" she called back, pinned a wet towel to the line, then came around to the front of the cottage wiping her hands on her apron. "The children are always a bit scared of strangers at first," she said with a smile, "but they'll be friendly enough later on, never fear."

Kristy felt she should introduce herself. "I'm Christine Henderson and this is my brother, Sam," she said.

"I know." The woman shook hands with a grip icy cold from the wet laundry. "I'm Rena O'Malley," she said in a friendly fashion. "It's great altogether to have the castle open over the Christmas season. Usually the place is closed up tighter than a drum this time of year."

"It's nice to be here," Kristy said, although she was beginning to wonder what they would all find to do for the next fortnight. Once Christmas was over she supposed they would crowd into the cars and go on excursions, but the absence of companions her own age made her concerned that the days might drag.

Sam was less foresighted. As he and his sister walked on, new vistas of adventure continued to open before his sparkling eyes. "Let's find out if there's a key to the tower door," he proposed. "Maybe there's a way of getting up to the roof!"

This project was one in which Grandpa thought all the adults might want to join, so everyone was rounded up except Grandma, whom nobody could find.

"Perhaps she's downstairs consulting with the cook," suggested Aunt Irene, as she knelt on the floor to bundle Ned into a snowsuit.

"I'll go down and see," Kristy offered obligingly. She had felt rather bashful about visiting the kitchen for no good reason. This errand offered an admirable excuse.

She found her grandmother sitting on a high stool,

talking with an ample, aproned woman with long straight hair pinned in an old-fashioned bun on top of her head.

"I don't think you've met Mrs. Quinn, dear."

"My, but you're a lucky lady to have such a fine granddaughter, God bless her," said the cook with a friendly smile.

Kristy explained the plans afoot, and her grandmother answered, "That sounds like fun, and I'll come right along. Give us just two more minutes to decide about Christmas dinner. Now let's see, Mrs. Quinn, you said you thought you might be able to get a goose?"

"Two geese, I should think, madam, if the gentlemen are hearty eaters."

"Fine. And for vegetables?"

"At this time of year we haven't much choice in the country. Potatoes, of course. And turnips are nice."

Kristy wrinkled her nose and Mrs. Quinn burst out laughing. "You wait until you taste my turnips!" she cried.

"What about dessert?"

"I've baked a Christmas cake for you to nibble on at tea," replied the cook, and went over to a cupboard to lift the lid on a container holding a huge confection with stiff white icing and paper decorations. "But I was thinking a homemade plum pudding would be lovely. Though for the recipe I like best I'd need a cup of whiskey and a pint of stout."

44

"That shouldn't be too difficult to arrange," Mrs. Henderson said, and while the two women settled the final details of the feast Kristy explored the big kitchen, with its freshly painted white plaster walls and blue cabinets, its chopping block, central work table, and shining black coal stove. The ovens looked big enough to roast half a dozen geese, if need be!

"But where's the sink?" she asked when the conversation seemed to have terminated.

"In the scullery. Come, I'll show you." Mrs. Quinn waddled cheerfully through a door into a room lined with dish closets and counters holding the heavy Irish silver that shone on the dining table at every meal. There was a big soapstone sink with wooden drainboards and off in the corner a cold closet that apparently took the place of a refrigerator. Here the quantity of meat, eggs, butter, milk, and other perishables made Kristy's eyes widen. "There's enough to feed an army!" she gasped.

"Remember, we're a dozen in all," her grandmother said, then cut Kristy's inspection short. "Come on, sweetie. The others will be getting impatient."

The others were, in fact, all gathered outside the tower door, while Fergus, looking fully as dour as he had yesterday, was removing the bar. The key was easy to find on the ring he carried because it was six times the size of any other, black with age, and looked as though it had been used for centuries.

45

"As indeed it has," remarked Fergus when someone made this comment. "Nobody knows for certain, but it could be well on to nine hundred years."

The door creaked open on a dim, square anteroom from which an ancient wooden staircase curved upward past a narrow perpendicular window set into the thick wall. Garden chairs were stacked in a corner, along with several pairs of rubber boots, a canvas umbrella, and some rotting baskets. From an ancient Maypole leaning in another corner, dozens of dusty, tattered ribbons fell in a tangle from a crown of faded paper flowers.

"Not much here but junk nowadays," Fergus vouchsafed.

"Is it safe to go upstairs?" asked Kristy's mother, glancing up the rotting staircase toward the second floor.

"Yes'm, there's four flights to the ramparts but look where you're going," Fergus replied glumly. "Some of the risers are shaky and you'd best stay toward the center of the halls."

Sam, who had bounded ahead, was told to wait by his father. He did so reluctantly. Obviously he had been fancying himself as an explorer, and wanted to be the first man to reach the uncharted shore above.

Fergus stood and watched the group start up the steps, but made no move to follow. "Just pull the door to when you leave," he called. "I'll lock up later on."

Kristy trailed along hopefully with the rest, but the big

room on the second floor was scarcely more interesting than the first. A ping-pong table, shabby and covered with dust, stood in the middle of the floor, laden with rows of rusted fishing flies, and nets, poles, hooks, and tongs hung from the ceiling or were piled in the deep window embrasures. Grandma winkled her nose distastefully. A scent of stale fish seemed to rise above the musty odor of the tower's interior like a whiff of lethal gas.

The third floor was occupied primarily by cobwebs, with which a tumbled stack of French and English fashion journals kept company—"L'Arte de la Mode," "London Fashion Album," "La Mode Nouvelle," and "Godey's Lady's Book," all a century old, with yellow, brittle pages that were fly-specked and mildewed beyond repair.

Only the Great Room on the top floor gave an indication of the tower's former magnificence. There was a heavy beamed ceiling, a baronial fireplace fully ten feet in width, and a parquet floor. An enormous chair, with carved oak arms and worn tapestry upholstery, stood before the hearth. Kristy went over and sat in it, her feet hanging well clear of the floor. What a giant of a man must once have found this a comfortable resting place!

The view from the roof was sufficiently spectacular, however, to have made the climb worthwhile. Over the treetops the Blackwater was visible for a mile or more, winding to Fermoy and on to County Waterford. The wan sunshine picked out the white backs of sheep grazing in the meadows and highlighted the spotted hides of a herd of cows being driven down a lane toward pastures on the riverbank.

Uncle Robert had brought along a pair of binoculars, which he passed around generously, but Kristy shook her head when he offered them to her. She was satisfied to stand in a slanting shaft of sunlight and drink in the colors of the peaceful landscape. She tried to imagine what life in the castle must have been like when it had been an Irish house-fortress with a big staff of servants, riding horses in the stables, and carriages carrying the landed gentry of County Cork through the tall iron gates. She furnished the rooms with damasks, the ladies and gentlemen with laces and velvets, but wondered how they ever managed to keep warm in the wintertime. Hot bricks could scarcely take the place of the electric blankets with which guests at the castle were provided in these modern times.

Leaning on her elbows on the parapet's broad coping, Kristy let her thoughts slide back and forth from the past to the present. Romantic as a wild boar roasted on the great fireplace spit might seem, the prospect of Christmas dinner cooked by Mrs. Quinn on the ample coal stove was more inviting. Yes, there were many advantages to being alive in the twentieth century.

The others drifted back downstairs by two and threes, but Kristy lingered, staring out over the river and idly watching a donkey emerge from an overgrown lane on the opposite bank. Strapped to his back were bags filled with something that couldn't be very heavy, because the slight animal, driven by a man with a short stick, stepped along briskly, although he was carrying a load almost twice his size.

From somewhere on the castle grounds, down in the direction of the boathouse, came a whistle that resembled a birdcall, yet had a piercing quality of its own. The driver paused and seemed to peer across the stream, then made a signal with a raised arm and turned the beast toward a copse of trees that bordered the broad meadows.

"Kristy! Coming, dear?"

"Right away, Mother."

"Close the door behind you."

"I will!"

As Kristy ran down the spiral stairs, without a second glance at the musty rooms, a bat flew in through a window opening and fluttered crazily above her head. She clutched her hair and pounded on, suddenly frightened, as though the ghosts of all the old castles in Ireland had materialized, storming Ballyhooly, rushing down from the tower battlements to subdue the cheerful American invaders who dared threaten their age-old demesne.

Outside, in the courtyard, a council was being held on the subject (introduced by Sam) of acquiring a Christmas tree. Uncle Robert favored going to Fermoy and looking

49

for a stand or a shop where such things were sold, but Kristy's father—an old hand by now at Irish ways—claimed that Miss Bessie Donovan was right; the only possibility of finding one was through Fergus. The grandparents were inclined to agree, so Sam was sent off to find the gardener, last seen going in the direction of the boathouse with a pitchfork in his hand.

Meanwhile, everyone talked about possible decorations. The Stephen Hendersons had brought a string of lights and a couple of boxes of Christmas tree balls from Dublin, but these wouldn't make much of a show. Kristy suggested that they make paper chains and popcorn garlands.

"Popcorn?" her mother queried. "The Irish are potato eaters. Where will you get any corn to pop?"

"In Fermoy," said Grandpa stubbornly. "Come on, Kristy. We'll drive to town and see what we can find!"

Two hours later, discouraged and empty-handed, Kristy and her grandfather got back to the castle. Apparently the only holiday decorations the local people found attractive were paper flowers and streamers. No evergreens, no holly, no tinsel, no Christmas tree balls or popcorn were for sale.

Meanwhile, Sam had found Fergus on the riverbank near the boathouse, and the gardener had promised to do the best he could to get a proper tree. He had gone off in the pickup truck, heading toward the Nagles Mountains, but had not yet returned.

50

By the time lunch was cleared away the sun had disappeared behind a bank of purple clouds, so the adults decided that the nap prescribed for Ned would be a good idea for everyone. Kristy and Sam were the lone dissenters. They wandered the grounds, exploring the gardens and mossy graveyard, investigating the salmon smokehouse in a small tower behind the kitchens, skidding and sliding down a rocky path to the padlocked boathouse, and walking the walls that enclosed the castle park. By teatime they were cold and tired, quite ready to settle down in front of a fire with the rest of the family and watch the winter twilight creep down from the hills. Kristy lay on her stomach on the hearth rug, turning the pages of a book she had bought in Dublin, but not really trying to read. She was thinking about the pages missing from the book on Irish castles. Suddenly she leaped to her feet. She'd go ask Nora if she knew why they could possibly have been torn out.

On the way through the hall, however, she was waylaid by Fergus, who stood in the main doorway with his cap in his hand. "Please tell your grandfather, Miss Kristy, that I got him a Christmas tree of sorts, and I'll put it up in the morning, wherever he says."

It was the longest speech Fergus had yet delivered in Kristy's presence, and before she could recover from her surprise he was gone, slipping back through the door like a wraith and closing it softly behind him. Abandoning her errand, Kristy hurried back to the drawing room. "Guess what! Fergus got us a Christmas tree," she cried.

"Wonderful!" Her grandmother clapped her hands happily. "We'll decorate it tomorrow, in time for Christmas eve."

Sam wanted to go see it at once, but at that moment the dinner bell rang, and everyone trooped into the dining room. Afterward he got involved in a game of chess with his Uncle Robert and forgot all about his impatience.

Aunt Irene, curled up on the couch with a sketch pad, had been making a crayon drawing of the chess players, their bent heads caught in the flickering firelight. Kristy peered over her shoulder admiringly. "Do you know how to make gravestone rubbings?" she asked.

"Yes. Why?"

"There's a marvelous old stone down in the little cemetery beyond the garden," Kristy said. "It's got a picture of a man blowing a trumpet and some writing in Gaelic."

"Gabriel, perhaps?" her aunt asked, holding her sketch off and considering it critically.

"Maybe. You ought to come take a look, tomorrow morning."

"I'd like that, Kristy."

"Fine! Right after breakfast?"

Aunt Irene nodded. "You be my guide."

"You'd better wear old shoes," Kristy warned. "It's wet and slippery."

The day before Christmas arrived on the heels of a bitterly cold dawn. Kristy dressed quickly, pulling on a pair of old slacks, sneakers, and an Aran Island sweater that had been her sixteenth birthday present, and raced Sam for the bathroom they shared with their parents.

All three bathrooms were situated at the end of a long hall, nowhere near any of the bedrooms, and each had the chill taken off by an electric heater affixed high on the wall. Nobody was tempted to linger, least of all Kristy and Sam.

For breakfast there was fresh homemade bread—the famous Irish loaf made of cracked wheat—along with canned fruit juice, prunes, and sausages and eggs kept hot over an alcohol flame. The men were already eating when Kristy came into the dining room, but the women had not yet arrived. Each person served himself, so the meal was very informal, in contrast to lunch or dinner.

Pouring some juice from a pitcher, Kristy picked up her glass and wandered over to the window, contemplating the wintry scene without. Below the garden the river meadows were tufted and crisp with hoarfrost, and a pair of sea gulls, blown inland, were wheeling above the water mistrustfully. Otherwise the landscape was empty. No cars or carts were crossing the bridge, no schoolchildren came running down from the hills, no bicyclists emerged from the side roads. For such a small country, Kristy was thinking, Ireland could be a very lonely place.

She poured a cup of hot tea, then helped herself to sausage and eggs, while her aunt brought Ned into the room and got him seated and started on his breakfast. Ned was always full of high spirits in the morning. His eyes sparkled, his smile flashed, and his vocabulary was extended to its fullest. Delighted at seeing Sam, who had become his idol, he carried on a conversation that effectively dampened any competition from the grown-ups.

His mother found the child far more interested in talking than in eating, and finally gave up. "You take over, Robert," she said to her husband. "Kristy and I are going to look at an old gravestone. We'll be back in fifteen minutes or so."

"Wrap up well, dear. It's a bitter morning," said Kristy's mother when she met her coming along the hall.

"Yes, Mother, I will."

The exchange was automatic and quite meaningless. Kristy didn't even put a coat over her sweater, although she did fling a scarf around her neck. "It's this way, through the rock garden." Leading her aunt, she hurried along the path, crunching dead leaves underfoot. Spiky firethorn, dotted with frosted red berries, climbed up the tumbled stones, and laurel and holly stood stiff and still against the gray sky. Cedars had been planted at strategic intervals, forming a dense background for plants long out of flower. Although the geranium plants had been frost-bitten in the night, a single Christmas rose opened its burgundy-red blossom to the pale winter light.

Aunt Irene bent to inspect it and murmured *"Helleborus niger.* Such an ugly botanical name for such an interesting plant." Sam came running up, boisterously brushed past his sister, and raced ahead.

Kristy heaved a profound sigh. "Once—just once!—I wish he'd stop following me around."

Ahead, tucked into the hillside, lay the small graveyard, overgrown with weeds, the thin stones leaning crazily this way and that. Sam had reached the entrance gate already, and was pushing it back, when suddenly he stopped, stood motionless for a second, then backed off as though he were being filmed by a camera in slow motion.

Turning, he came walking on tiptoe toward his sister and his aunt. "There's a man in there," he said in a horrified whisper. "Lying on his face. He looks as if he's dead."

4

Sam's expression precluded any thought that he might be teasing. His eyes were big with shock, his skin chalky. Kristy stood hesitating on the path, but her aunt moved forward quickly, without speaking. Sam didn't follow. He came to Kristy and leaned against her, more like a small child than an eleven-year-old. "Honest," he said. "I think he's dead."

"I believe you." Kristy hugged her brother comfortingly, forgetting her recent annoyance, then said, "Run get Dad, and tell him to bring a blanket. I'll stay with Aunt Irene."

She would far rather have been heading toward the castle herself, but she was smitten by a sense of responsibility accompanying her sixteen years. Conquering a creeping feeling of repugnance, Kristy went along to the gate and stood holding it ajar, the rusty iron cold and rough against her warm palm.

Aunt Irene was bending over the prone figure of a slight man wearing hip boots, muddy corduroy trousers, and a tan canvas fishing jacket that had seen better days. Kristy watched her reach down and touch a hand emerging from the jacket sleeve, then straighten quickly. "He's quite cold," she said, glancing around at Kristy. "We'd better get the men."

"I've already sent Sam for Dad," Kristy said, and backed a pace away from the gate, looking hopefully toward the castle. Although she had caught only a glimpse of the back of the victim's head, there was something familiar about the sandy hair, bristly and ragged above the jacket collar. The man's face, buried in the fallen leaves, was quite invisible.

Then recognition suddenly hit her. "It looks like Fergus!" she gasped.

Aunt Irene nodded. "If he *is* dead, we mustn't touch him," she said, as though apologizing for a lack of compassion. Yet Kristy could see that her aunt's eyes were full of concern.

"Why not?"

"I don't know. I just remember—"

"Here they come!" Kristy beckoned frantically to her father and Uncle Robert, who came hurrying down the narrow path at a run. They were followed by her grandfather, moving at only a slightly slower pace.

The next few minutes would always remain to Kristy as sharp as a scene on television. Her father pounded past her, saying brusquely, "You'd better get back to the house," but although she nodded she couldn't seem to move. Without any of her aunt's compunction, the men spread the blanket on the ground and rolled the body over on it. At once Kristy's earlier suspicion was confirmed.

"It's Fergus," her father said, while Kristy shuddered at the sight of the gardener's forehead, clotted with dark, dried blood. Still, she couldn't seem to turn away. Her grandfather came up, put his arm briefly around her shoulders, and said, "Irene, take Kristy back inside. This is no place for a young girl."

"You should tell them not to touch the body," Aunt Irene said in a quavering voice. "You should call the police."

"Why don't *you* do that, dear?"

The suggestion worked, and got Kristy and her aunt moving along the trodden path.

"Could he have had a fall and hit his head on a gravestone?" Kristy asked as they reached the castle courtyard.

"I don't know." Aunt Irene sounded troubled and uncertain.

"Maybe he isn't dead. Maybe he's just badly hurt." Kristy wanted to be hopeful, but she knew, even as she

58

spoke, that she was talking nonsense. Although she had never before seen a corpse, there was no mistaking the pallor, the stillness of that face.

Aunt Irene shook her head, as though no reply were necessary. She went straight to the telephone in the drawing room, saying to the operator, "There's been an accident at the castle. Can you get me the police?"

There was a pause. Then she said, "I beg your pardon. What do you call them? Guards, did you say?"

"*Gardai,*" said Kristy, and spelled it. "*G-a-r-d-a-i.*"

"Yes, I'll need a doctor. And is there a local priest we could call?" Turning from the phone, she told Kristy's mother and grandmother, who were standing with Ned by the window, looking out toward the hidden graveyard, "The nearest police station is in Fermoy."

After another pause a man's voice rasped over the wire, and Aunt Irene enlarged on the explanation she had made to the telephone operator. "I'm calling from Ballyhooly Castle. There's been a serious accident to the gardener, Fergus O'Malley. He may even be dead. I'll call a doctor at once, but can you get someone over here right away?"

"It seems to me you're putting the cart before the horse," Kristy's grandmother said. "Shouldn't you have phoned the doctor first, Irene dear?"

Irene glanced at Sam, who had recovered his equilibrium. "I doubt if a doctor will be able to do much good," she murmured as she turned back to the phone.

59

"I told you he was dead," Sam said aggressively.

"Sh, dear!" said his grandmother gently. "You have a job to do, and that's to take care of Ned, while Aunt Irene tries to reach a doctor. Please act grown-up now. You can be a big help."

"I already was. I found him, didn't I?"

"Somebody should break the news to Mrs. O'Malley," said his mother, ignoring Sam.

"Not until we're sure!" objected Kristy. She was thinking of the five little faces at the cottage window, and knew that this would be the hardest task of all.

"I'd better go find Nora," Grandma said. "After all, she's in charge here." She went out of the room swiftly, shutting the door behind her, and Kristy could hear her heels clattering along the hall floor.

In the meantime her aunt was consulting the telephone operator, who turned out to be the postmistress, Bessie Donovan.

"The family uses Dr. Harrison in Mallow," repeated Aunt Irene with her hand over the receiver. "By the family I assume Miss Donovan means the owners. Anyway, she's trying to get in touch with the doctor at his office. She says to hold the wire."

The telephone emitted a series of unexpected noises. It coughed and sputtered with accents that were almost human. Wires whirred, bells rang, and the hand crank attached to the old-fashioned box seemed to run amok.

Finally, however, the connection was made and the doctor apprised of the gravity of the situation. "He says he'll drive over as soon as he has seen a waiting patient." Aunt Irene put down the receiver with a sigh of relief. "He sounded nice."

Although barely five minutes had gone by, it seemed an eternity to Kristy. "Before anybody tells Mrs. O'Malley, why don't I invite the children up here to play?" she asked with a flash of inspiration. "Sam, you and Ned can help, can't you?" She fixed her brother with a stern and commanding glance.

"I can help," Sam answered rather truculently. "I don't know about Neddie here." At that moment Ned, quite oblivious to the crisis in which the household was caught up, was attempting to tumble Sam on the floor. He came rushing at him in a series of headlong dives, shouting and crowing. Sam made futile attempts to defend himself, but at least he was distracted from grim reality.

"I think that's a marvelous idea," her grandmother was saying. "Hurry, Kristy, before the men come back. And don't say anything at all about the accident. Let Grandpa and the others take care of that."

Kristy nodded, understanding and agreeing. She dashed across the courtyard and found Mrs. O'Malley shepherding the five children out of the cottage door. "Even if it's a bit chilly," she was saying to the eldest, "you all need some fresh air."

"Could I take them up to the castle?" Kristy asked rather breathlessly. "Sam and Ned—that's my three-year-old-cousin—would love to have somebody to play with. Could I, please?"

Mrs. O'Malley looked surprised and doubtful. "They've never been inside the castle," she said. "I'm not sure they'd know how to behave."

The children stood by, silent and equally uncertain, but Kristy was insistent. "I promise I'll bring them right home unless they're very, very good," she said with a courageous smile. "Now, tell me your names, and I'll try to remember." So that she wouldn't have to meet their mother's unsuspecting eyes she crouched on the ground near the youngest. "You must be almost Ned's age. Can you talk?"

The little girl, a towhead with strawberry cheeks, put a finger in her mouth and stared at Kristy with alarmed blue eyes. "That's Breeda," said her mother. "Speak up, child!" But Breeda remained tongue-tied in front of the stranger who had unexpectedly appeared in their midst.

Brian was Breeda's twin brother, Ormond was five, Dagan seven, and the eldest, a dark-haired, slender nine-year-old girl with eyes the color of gentians and an alabaster complexion, was named Rosaleen. Kristy shook hands gravely with each of the children, and as quickly as possible persuaded them to come with her to the castle. She was right in thinking that their curiosity would overcome their timidity.

At the entrance door, however, the children almost bolted. Two round, iridescent tears appeared on Breeda's lower lids and slid down to the curve of her plump cheeks, there to tremble indefinitely.

"Oh, come on, don't be a big silly," Dagan urged, and caught the toddler's hand, pulling her over the threshold and into the house. The rest followed, and Kristy led them at once to the drawing room, where she introduced them to her mother and grandmother, then to Sam and Ned.

During this entire time the little O'Malleys remained speechless, but Ned was charmed by the newcomers. He ran around Breeda in narrowing circles, and finally reached out and touched her, obviously delighted to learn that she was real.

Rosaleen, the eldest of the O'Malleys, knew her manners. She perched on the edge of the long sofa, and her younger brothers and sisters joined her, forming a tight, straight line with Breeda on the far end.

Ned apparently thought this was some kind of game, because he squeezed in beside Breeda, chortling happily and admiring everything about his new acquaintance, from the blue ribbon tying a few wisps of her shoulder-length hair on top of her head to the red sneakers on her tiny feet.

Breeda's twin brother Brian was examining Ned surreptitiously but with almost as much enthusiasm as the

American child had shown. After each of the visitors had been given a cooky, the three youngest relaxed and started to tumble around on the floor like a trio of puppies. Sam, true to his promise to help, began to teach Ormond and Dagan to play Parcheesi, while Kristy took Rosaleen to her bedroom to show her the Irish Christmas tree decorations her parents had brought from Dublin.

From the east window the graveyard was visible, but Kristy maneuvered her young guest into a position where she could see neither the path approaching it nor the copse of trees sheltering the white stones. She chattered along at a great rate, determined to keep Rosaleen diverted, although her curiosity kept mounting with every passing minute. What could be happening outside?

Had the *gardai* arrived from Fermoy? Had her father and uncle managed to carry Fergus along the path and across the courtyard to the cottage? And if so, how had poor Mrs. O'Malley reacted to the tragedy? By now Kristy was no longer trying to convince herself that the gardener might still be alive. She accepted the verdict of her own eyes and rearranged her throughts accordingly.

Rosaleen was unaware of Kristy's divided attention. She moved around the room quietly, touching the quilted bedspread, running her fingers over the polished wood of an antique table, examining the snapshots tucked into the mirror above the bureau. At a picture of a tall boy with a tennis racket under his arm she paused. "Who's that?" she asked. "A friend of yours?"

"Yes," Kristy said. "His name is Michael Curtis, and he goes to school with me in Dublin. We play tennis together sometimes."

"He's good-looking," said Rosaleen, more out of politeness than an interest in the opposite sex.

Kristy nodded, agreeing. "Michael has an aunt in Fermoy, where he visits sometimes." She was wishing that sometimes were now.

"Do you know many boys?" Rosaleen asked.

The question seemed strange to Kristy. "Quite a few," she replied. "Why?"

"Boys don't stay around Ballyhooly long after they're sixteen," said Rosaleen. "They can't get jobs here, so they go to a city like Cork or Dublin."

"Have you ever been to Dublin?" Kristy asked.

"No, but I've been to Cork."

"Dublin's much larger. My father is teaching at the university there."

"I know," said Rosaleen. "Uncle Fergus told me."

Kristy blinked in astonishment. "Uncle *who?*" she shrilled.

"Uncle Fergus. You know, he's the gardener here."

"But I thought he was your father!" Kristy gasped.

For the first time since she had entered the castle Rosaleen actually laughed. "Oh, no!" she said. "Mama's just keeping house for him while Papa is moving his bicycle shop to Cork. We'll be going to live there sometime in January."

Relief made Kristy weak. She sank down on the edge of the bed, clasped her her hands and murmured, "But that's marvelous, perfectly marvelous!"

"What is? Living in Cork?"

"Yes, that too." Kristy jumped up and caught Rosaleen's hand. "Come on back to the living room. I've got to tell the others right away."

Althought the fire was burning merrily, the big room was empty. Children's voices could be heard, however, drifting up the stairwell from the kitchen. Apparently Sam had taken his charges downstairs to beg another round of cookies from Mrs. Quinn. They were just about to come up again when Kristy leaned over the bannister.

"Where's Mother?" she called.

"Gone out with Grandma and Aunt Irene. You know where." Sam sounded both mysterious and full of pride that he had been given command over his young companions.

"Rosaleen, you stay with Sam and help take care of the little ones. I'll be right back." Kristy tore out of the house, across the cold stones of the court, and down the carriage drive to the cottage by the gate, where a group of men huddled near two strange cars. Neither Mrs. O'Malley nor any of the women from the castle were in sight.

Kristy stopped short. She had no business barging into the cottage, where Fergus undoubtedly had been taken, but she needed to share her relief at Rosaleen's disclosure.

Scarcely able to contain herself, she wanted to shout the news.

Clustered near the road, the men—her father, uncle, and grandfather among them—had their heads together in a conference so absorbing that they hadn't noticed her appearance in the drive. Kristy had to go up and actually tug at her father's sleeve before he became aware of her presence. Then he broke away from the group with a frown. "What are you doing out here?"

"I've got to tell you something!" Kristy whispered. "Fergus O'Malley wasn't the children's father. He was their uncle!" Quite involuntarily, she used the past tense.

At that moment Mrs. O'Malley appeared in the cottage doorway, her face flushed and her plump shoulders covered by a shawl. She dabbed at her eyes with a handkerchief while she followed the three American women to the front steps, but Kristy apprehended shock and horror in her expression rather than any deeply felt grief.

Thanking the ladies for their concern, she spoke in a perfectly natural, open manner. Then she said a truly surprising thing. "He was a stubborn man and a hard one, my brother-in-law Fergus, but who would want to do a dastardly thing like that?"

5

Murder?

Was Mrs. O'Malley suggesting that Fergus might have
been murdered? Kristy could hardly believe her ears!
However, there was something about the sharpness with
which her father had spoken, something in her mother's
manner at this very moment, as she glanced around and
saw Kristy standing there, that indicated unusual concern.
Both of her parents were bent on protecting her from the
ugly suspicion, but it was too late. Mrs. O'Malley's question had put an entirely new aspect on the gardener's
death.

Inevitably, Kristy found herself reliving the scene in the
graveyard, after Sam had been sent running for his father.
Aunt Irene had said something rather curious, which the
men later ignored. "We mustn't touch him," she kept

repeating. Now, of course, it made sense. Aunt Irene must have suspected murder from the first. A detective story fan, she would have realized immediately that the scene of a possible crime must be left undisturbed.

Even Kristy had read enough mysteries—and certainly she had seen enough television shows—to know the rules of the game. This, however, was no game. One couldn't flick a switch or shut a book and make the vision of the gardener's body, face down on the frosty ground, disappear.

Aunt Irene came over to where Kristy was standing, linked an arm through hers, and led her determinedly back toward the castle.

"You suspected all along, didn't you?" Kristy asked.

"Maybe. Or maybe I'm just naturally cautious. However, it's only a possibility, Kristy. It's not even a probability, actually. The police are almost certain to call it accidental death."

"He *could* have had a fall and hit his head, then?"

"Of course," said Aunt Irene. "And it's very likely that's just the way it happened. After all, as Mrs. O'Malley said, who would want to do a thing like that?"

"He wasn't a very attractive man," Kristy said slowly. "He might have had enemies."

Aunt Irene shrugged. "We mustn't spoil our holiday by dwelling on it, Kristy. And if I were you I wouldn't men-

69

tion the possibility of murder to Sam. Children that age are so impressionable."

Kristy was flattered to be included, by inference, among the grown-ups, and she agreed readily, although privately she doubted that Sam could be kept in the dark for long. He was here, there, and everywhere, active as a dragonfly, and sooner or later he was bound to overhear some gossip among the servants or the villagers, if not in the family group.

At the moment, however, he was still acting as general of his juvenile army. He had dressed Ned in a snow jacket and brought him along outside with the five O'Malleys. All of them were standing in front of the stables, looking up at a Christmas tree they had discovered leaning against the wall.

To Kristy's eyes it was a sad looking specimen, tall and spare, with short, ragged branches jutting out at intervals from a crooked trunk. She thought of the beautiful Douglas firs in Oregon with a wave of homesickness, and wondered where the gardener had managed to find such a spindly tree. It scarcely seemed worth setting up in the house at all.

Sam, however, appeared unaware of its ugliness. "Do you think it will fit or will we have to cut off the top?" he called to his sister and his aunt as they approached.

"You'd better ask your grandmother," said Aunt Irene, while she and Kristy waited for the other two women to come up.

"It isn't exactly a thing of beauty," Grandma said appraisingly. "Turn it around, Sam. It must have a good side. There!"

Kristy couldn't see that one side was any better than the other, but she realized that Sam and the older O'Malleys were relieved by her grandmother's qualified approval. They were seeing the tree not as it was but as it should—and possibly could—be.

"Let's put it at the end of the entrance hall so that it can be seen from the front door," suggested Grandma.

"Not in the living room?" Sam asked.

"With the open fire, that could be dangerous," Aunt Irene reminded him.

Sam didn't argue the point. "When can we decorate it?"

"What about before dinner this evening?" his grandmother suggested.

So remote a time made Sam lose interest in the project. He let the tree fall back against the stone wall and spoke to Kristy. "You going to take care of these kids now?"

Rosaleen backed away, looking offended, but the younger children didn't seem to object to Sam's manner. Aside from Ned and Brian, who were chasing each other busily around the perimeter of the group, they regarded her hopefully.

At this juncture, however, Mrs. O'Malley came along the driveway, a shawl thrown over her head and her thick-soled shoes crunching on the loose stones. "I thank you kindly for all your trouble," she said to Kristy and Sam, "but it's quite all right. They can come with me now."

Breeda, in fact, had already run to her mother and clutched at her skirts, from where she peered back at Ned and Brian, who were now tussling with each other on the ground.

"We'll be glad to keep the children here for the rest of the morning," said Aunt Irene. "Wouldn't that make things easier for you?"

At this suggestion Breeda burst into tears, thus settling the matter. All of the O'Malleys trooped over to their mother, who went off toward the cottage in their midst.

A few minutes later the men came back to the castle. "Everything's under control," Kristy's father said at once to the group once more gathered in the drawing room. "The undertaker has come and gone. Patrick O'Malley has been reached, and is taking the noon bus from Cork. He was coming home for Christmas anyway."

"There is one more thing to be got through," Uncle Robert put in, looking at his wife. "The police would like to ask you a few questions, Irene. You and Kristy and Sam, since you found him. It's only routine."

"I was the one who *really* found him," Sam bragged.

"Sh!" said his mother, shaking her head, while Kristy glanced at her brother and feigned a yawn, batting her lips with her fingertips.

"Well, I did!"

"Sam!" said his father sharply, and Sam subsided as Nora appeared in the drawing room door. "It's the *garda* from Fermoy, sir," she said to Kristy's grandfather. "Shall I show him in?"

The uniformed officer who entered the room seemed short and stocky next to the tall American men. He had a flat nose, full cheeks, curly black hair, and eyes that looked as though they would crinkle at the corners if he smiled.

He was not smiling now. With his mouth fixed in a serious line, he glanced at each of the nine strangers. Kristy's grandmother took the helm and introduced him all around, which seemed to give him confidence. "I hope you'll excuse me," he said "for barging in on you like this —the day before Christmas and all."

"We understand," said Kristy's grandfather. "You want to talk to Mrs. Russell and my grandchildren, don't you? Would you like the rest of us to leave?"

The constable appeared to weigh this question carefully. "Now that you're here, you might as well stay," he decided, although he looked doubtfully at Ned.

"I'll just ask Nora if she'll give the baby some milk and crackers," suggested Aunt Irene. She took Ned by the hand and went down the hall, then reappeared almost at once.

Everyone found places to sit. Kristy settled herself on one of the Chippendale side chairs, where she felt unnaturally straight and stiff. Sam perched on the arm of the overstuffed sofa next to his mother, and the *garda*, whose name was Sergeant Walsh, sat on a stool beside a big round table, got out a notebook and the chewed stub of a yellow pencil. He started by addressing Aunt Irene.

"Mrs. Russell, I understand you were the one, with the two young people here, who found—er, excusing the phrase—the body."

Sam glared at his aunt and waited for her reply, then relaxed visibly when she said, "Actually, it was my nephew who discovered a man lying face down just inside the graveyard gate. Sam had run on ahead of Kristy and me."

"What made you happen to go to the graveyard, may I ask, on such a chilly morning?"

"My niece was interested in showing me a carving on an old gravestone. She thought I might like to take a rubbing."

"A rubbing?" Sergeant Walsh scratched his head with his pencil. He looked dubious. "What's that?"

"It's a way of transferring a design from stone to a piece of paper. You do it with friction," Aunt Irene tried to explain.

"Did you have the paper with you?" the policeman asked.

"No, we were just going to take a look at the gravestone. I planned to work on it later, if it appealed to me."

Sergeant Walsh frowned, obviously considering this young woman slightly fey, talking about an *appealing* gravestone.

"O.K., so the boy had gone on ahead. How did he react when he saw Fergus O'Malley just lying there?"

"He didn't know it was Fergus, Sergeant Walsh, because he couldn't see the face. He was startled, of course" —Aunt Irene glanced at Sam—"and maybe a little frightened. He just backed off and said something like 'There's a man lying on the ground. Maybe he's dead.'"

Kristy fully expected the *garda* to turn to Sam at this point, but apparently he planned to question each person in turn. "What happened next, Mrs. Russell?"

"Sam came out of the gate, and Kristy sent him back to the house to fetch his father, while I went on inside the little cemetery. I thought Fergus might have had a fall and been hurt."

"Fergus? What made you think of Fergus? You just said you didn't know who the man was."

"I said *Sam* didn't know. Naturally I thought of Fergus, especially when I saw he was wearing a fishing jacket and hip boots. Who else would be likely to be on the castle grounds at that time of morning, except the gardener?"

Sergeant Walsh obviously regarded this remark as a statement rather than a question. "Did you touch the body, Mrs. Russell?"

An involuntary shudder made Aunt Irene's shoulder's twitch. "Yes. I bent down and felt the wrist for a pulse."

"But you didn't turn him over?"

"Not I!" Aunt Irene replied promptly. "In all the detective stories I've ever read the author makes the point that a body should be left undisturbed until the police get there. When the men arrived, they had no such scruples," she added with a transient smile.

Kristy glanced at her father and her uncle, who both looked glum, then at her grandfather, who seemed mildly entertained by his daughter's reply. The sergeant, however, was shaking his head again.

"You were right, Mrs. Russell, quite right." He looked at the men severely. "The ground was trampled, the body was carted off, the gate was pulled and pushed to and fro by half a dozen people. It's as though you were all conspiring to give the *gardai* a hard time!"

"That's nonsense," said Kristy's grandfather unexpectedly. "My son and son-in-law merely did the natural and humane thing. How many people who've met with an accident are left undisturbed until the police arrive? Not one in a hundred, I'll bet."

This outburst threw Sergeant Walsh off base for a full twenty seconds. He chewed his pencil abstractedly but didn't attempt to argue. Instead he turned to Sam.

"You confirm everything your aunt has told me, young man?"

"I—what?"

"Confirm. You agree it's true?"

"Sure, why not?" asked Sam with a puzzled expression. "Aunt Irene wouldn't fib."

Kristy stifled a nervous impulse to chuckle. If Sam should be counted rude, she knew it was quite unintentional, although he might be disappointed if he weren't allowed to repeat the story his aunt had just told.

Fortunately, Sergeant Walsh said, "Suppose you tell me about what happened in your own way."

"Well, you see it's like this." Sam leaned forward, obviously pleased to be the center of attention. "I was first through the gate, like Aunt Irene said, and there was this man on the ground, just lying there, looking dead—"

"Had you ever seen a dead man before?" the constable interrupted.

"Well, no, naturally. But you could just sort of tell—"

"How could you tell?" asked Sergeant Walsh. "Did you touch him?"

"Hey, are you kidding?" Sam yelped. "No *indeed!*"

"Did you notice anything special? Anything your aunt hasn't mentioned?"

Sam became thoughtful. "Yeah, one thing," he said after a moment. "He wasn't wearing a cap and Fergus always had a cap on. You know, Dad, that brown cloth thing."

His father nodded. "Not that it proves anything. We met Fergus for the first time when we arrived in Ballyhooly the day before yesterday," he added for Sergeant Walsh's benefit.

The Sergeant scrawled something in his notebook, while Kristy sat and pondered the strangeness of fate and the crowding of events into the past few hours. Was it only yesterday she had been craving a little excitement? She certainly had her wish, although it was not of the kind she might have bargained for.

"Well, miss, do you have anything to add?"

"N-not really." Startled from her reverie, Kristy felt self-conscious. "Except, why would Fergus have on hip boots? Yesterday, working in the garden, he was wearing regular work shoes, the high kind, something like those you have on now."

The *garda* looked down at his shoes, surprised to find them the center of attention, then unexpectedly flushed and tucked his feet modestly under the stool. "These aren't the boots I generally wear on duty," he explained. "I got the call from Ballyhooly at home, and hopped right over without bothering to change."

Having made this unnecessary explanation, Sergeant Walsh turned his attention to the three men, trying to ascertain whether any of them thought it probable that Fergus could have tripped on a vine or even a rabbit snare and thus cracked his head on a tombstone.

It was their concerted opinion that this was unlikely, because neither piece of evidence had turned up at the scene. "The thing *I* can't understand," said Kristy's father, "is what he was doing in the graveyard. The gardens are all neatly tended, the paths raked, and the bushes trimmed, but that patch of ground where we found him hasn't been touched in years."

"Maybe he was just starting to work on it," suggested Sam irrepressibly.

Kristy was scornful. "Don't be silly. He didn't have a rake or anything with him, did he?"

"I suppose there will be an autopsy?" asked Aunt Irene.

Sam opened his mouth, no doubt to ask "What's that?" but his mother put a hand on his knee and formed the word "Sh" with her lips, although she didn't make a sound.

"Of course," Sergeant Walsh said, and stood up. "Well, I guess that will be all, folks. I'd best go down and talk with Mrs. O'Malley."

He stuffed the notebook and his ravaged pencil into a coat pocket, then peered across the room to contemplate the scene beyond the big bay windows. Clouds were hanging low over the rim of mountains, and rain was spitting against the mullioned windowpanes. Below the descending terraces the meadow grass was green and the river flowed sluggishly among the alders and rushes. "Nice view you've got here," he said.

79

"We think so too." Grandma was the gracious hostess again. "It's a beautiful location for a castle."

Sergeant Walsh agreed. "All of ye have a merry Christmas," he said with a flickering smile. "And don't let this thing be on your minds." He hesitated a moment, then added, "It would be too bad to let poor O'Malley's misfortune ruin your holiday."

"It would indeed," agreed Grandma, lifting her chin. "It's the one time in our lives we'll all be together in an Irish castle, and I don't intend to let anything spoil it. Not *anything*!"

"That's the spirit," Sergeant Walsh approved, his mouth curling into a grin, his eyes predictably crinkling at the corners. He made a mock salute, about-faced, and marched to the door. Then he paused and turned, as though struck by an afterthought.

Pointing a finger first at Sam, then at Kristy, he said severely, "And don't you youngsters go listening to the gossip in the village, hear? There's no ghost at Ballyhooly who'd be giving Fergus O'Malley the time of day."

6

Sam croaked, "Ghost?"

"Sh! Sergeant Walsh was just teasing you, darling," his grandmother said. "Now not another word about poor Fergus O'Malley. We've got to get organized. Have you forgotten? Tonight is Christmas eve!"

For such a diminutive woman, Mrs. Henderson showed remarkable generalship. Steadfastly refusing to discuss the tragedy further, she dispatched messengers to Fermoy for all manner of things she considered necessary —an extra strand of Christmas tree lights, candles for the dinner table, flowers for a centerpiece, wine to accompany the goose. Immediately after lunch a foraging party started out in one of the cars, with Kristy and Sam along on a special assignment. The adults had all contributed to a fund with which to buy presents for the O'Malley chil-

81

dren, and Kristy was carrying two Irish pounds in her pocketbook.

"Let Sam help you choose little gifts for each of them," Grandma had suggested privately. "Get his mind off this thing as much as you can."

"I will," Kristy promised, although she was just as curious as her brother. How could anyone help but be? Nevertheless, she understood her grandmother's determination to make the holiday a merry one, and tried to do her part.

The shops lining Fermoy's main street were small and sparsely stocked compared to those in Dublin. Kristy and Sam wandered through half a dozen stores, selecting toys for Breeda and Brian, picture books for Ormond and Dagan, and a gay woolen scarf for Rosaleen. Wrapping paper and ribbon were more difficult to find. Sam became bored, gave up the chase, and went back to wait in the car for the others to return. Kristy, however, was more resolute. She hurried in and out of every likely door, and eventually found a roll of red tissue and a wheel of narrow white ribbon that would have to do.

The woman behind the counter, pink-cheeked and buxom, was waiting on another customer while Kristy made her selections. As she counted change into a man's rough palm, she said, "I suppose you've heard about Fergus O'Malley. A terrible thing, the day before Christmas and all."

The man nodded. "The Yanks at the castle found him

in the graveyard, it's said. I used to know Fergus quite well in the old days, but I can't say he was a fellow you'd take to. A mean man and a bitter one, I always thought."

"Still," said the storekeeper, "it was a bad way to end."

Kristy, from behind a row of shelves, listened unashamedly as the customer agreed. Then, quite surprisingly, he chuckled. "The folks round Ballyhooly will be blaming it on the ghost, like as not. I can just hear the lads in the pubs. All the old stories will be raked up and sorted over. What a time they'll have tonight!"

The woman behind the counter sniffed audibly. "Better they'd go to church and say their prayers than be standing at a bar drinking stout and talking claptrap. I hope you'll have the good sense to stay away, Liam McMurrough."

A mocking laugh was Liam's only reply. As he turned to leave the store he spotted Kristy and glanced at her briefly, no longer amused, with eyes unexpectedly wary. Under a cap set at a cocky angle over a shock of black hair, Kristy glimpsed a coarse-featured, youngish face with a stubble of beard half concealing a red welt that ran diagonally across one cheek. Not a fellow she'd like to meet on a dark road at night, she thought as the woman called, "Can I help you, miss?"

Kristy brought her wrapping materials to the counter. "I'd like this paper and ribbon. How much do I owe you?" she asked.

The woman named a sum and without comment made change for the ten shilling note Kristy handed her, although she certainly must have spotted the American girl as a stranger in town. "We're staying at Ballyhooly," Kristy ventured. "I couldn't help overhearing your conversation with the man who just left. What *is* the story about the ghost at the castle? We're all just dying to know."

Appearing embarrassed by such a direct question, the storekeeper shrugged. "All the castles hereabouts have legends of ghosts," she said primly. Then, her former loquacity quenched, she shut her mouth firmly, as though she were biting her tongue.

Any attempt at persuasion would be in vain, Kristy recognized at once. The ghost of Ballyhooly was apparently a local myth to be protected from overcurious foreigners. Accepting defeat gracefully, Kristy murmured something innocuous and said "Thank you," and "Merry Christmas."

"Many happy returns," the Irish woman responded as she left the store and started back to the car.

The streets of Fermoy were now almost deserted. Shops were closing early for the holiday, lights were being doused and metal shutters drawn tight down to the pavements. Into a food market near the bridge over the Blackwater went scurrying the last frantic customers, and on the road from Fermoy to Ballyhooly cars were skittering along like beetles in the gathering dusk.

The sky had turned bleak, and a flight of rooks swept past the castle tower like black snow as Kristy ran across the courtyard with her bundles. In the hall the skinny Christmas tree had been set up—a scarecrow of a tree, as anyone could see—but Grandma was indomitably stringing it with a first set of lights.

"Oh, there you are!" she cried. "Just in time. We've sawed off the top and wired the extra branches into the bare spaces. Don't you think it looks a lot better?"

"Yes, indeed," Kristy fibbed, although privately she felt sure that nothing could improve the skeletal outlines. By the time a second string of lights was added, however, she began to pretend, along with everyone else, that the tree would be quite satisfactory.

Indeed, after dark had fallen beyond the long French doors, the pine looked quite stately standing there hung with lights and a few shivering colored balls. The family members all brought the small presents they had crowded into their luggage and scattered them underneath the lowest branches. Both Nora and Mary came to admire the effect, and Grandma heaved a contented sigh.

"There," she said. "That will do very nicely, don't you think?"

Sam sniffed appreciatively and said, "It even smells like Christmas now." Then Ned worked his way downstairs, fanny first, from his parents' bedroom, and stood looking at the decorations in solemn wonder.

85

His grandmother bent and quickly scooped the child up into her arms. "Pretty?" she asked.

Ned nodded. "Pretty," he repeated, and crowed in delight, wriggling free to touch the bright ornaments.

Kristy held him back. "That's a no-no," she warned. "You can look all you like but you mustn't touch."

Ned was about to howl in protest when his mother came running downstairs. "Kristy's right," she said. "A Christmas tree is to look at, not to play with. Let's go see if we can find the truck you lost before lunch." Taking his hand, she led him persuasively toward the drawing room.

Sam followed, but Kristy went down to the warm, steamy kitchen on the ground floor, where Mrs. Quinn was chopping a head of cabbage and Mary had started to wash up the cups and saucers used for tea. A snapping, crackling sound, accompanied by the delicious smell of roasting meat, came from the oven, and on a counter top stood a rice pudding with a rich brown crust.

"Mmm!" Kristy murmured appreciatively, and won a smile of approval from the cook.

"One thing about Americans," she said. "They like to eat."

Kristy appropriated the high stool kept near the cupboards and pulled it over to the table, climbing onto it and wrapping her ankles around the legs. "Have you been the cook here for very long, Mrs. Quinn?" she asked conversationally.

"Going on twelve years."

"Then you must have known Mr. O'Malley pretty well?"

"As well as the next, I suppose. Though Fergus, God rest his soul, was never the talkative sort." Mrs. Quinn heaved an enigmatic sigh.

"Was he gardener here when you came, Mrs. Quinn?" probed Kristy.

The cook looked surprised. "Not Fergus. He was Colonel Henry's gillie until a couple of years ago."

"What's a gillie?" Kristy asked. It was the first time she had encountered the word, although she had been in Ireland nearly four months.

Mary called from the sink, "You never heard of a gillie? It's a man that takes care of a gentleman fisherman, rows the boat, and finds the best spots and all that."

"Fergus would have stayed a gillie right on through if the colonel hadn't sold out and gone back to England," Mrs. Quinn put in. "He'd be up with the larks and down at the river six days out of seven."

Mary turned from the sink, wiped her hands on her apron, and nodded solemnly. "Always declared a fortune could be made from the river, if a man had half a chance."

Kristy swung around on the stool and wondered aloud, "What could he have meant by that?"

Mrs. Quinn answered, "There's not a bit of telling. Fergus had peculiar ways. Not like his brother at all."

"Has Patrick come yet, I wonder?" asked Mary, whose hands on the blue china were as red as cockscombs.

"If he caught the noon bus from Cork he'll be here," Mrs. Quinn answered, "but the three o'clock is bound to be late on Christmas eve."

"You'll find Patrick O'Malley as different from Fergus as day is from night," Mary told Kristy. "He's a square, stout man with a hearty laugh that will tickle your ribs."

"Still, it will be a sad Christmas down at the cottage," Mrs. Quinn remarked as though talking to herself.

"We bought the children some presents when we went to Fermoy," Kristy said. "But we couldn't find any flowers for Grandma. Fresh ones, I mean. They said there were none closer than Cork."

Mrs. Quinn piled the chopped cabbage into a saucepan and confirmed that was very likely. "Fermoy and Mallow are poor towns, by city standards. The people hereabouts don't have the money to spend on winter posies that'll die in a day or two."

"It's a shame," put in Mary, "that we didn't know your grandma had a hankering for flowers. Just yesterday we cut the last of the geraniums in the garden to decorate the chapel."

"And not a day too soon," said Mrs. Quinn. "Last night there was a killing frost."

"I still can't get used to geraniums at Christmas," Kristy put in.

"Why not?" asked Mary, misunderstanding. "They're handy and they're red. Mixed in with holly they make a fine note of color for the services."

"Which reminds me that Nora must tell the madam the time church starts," said Mrs. Quinn, bending to pull a pan of fresh rolls from the oven. "Some of the family may want to go."

Aside from Aunt Irene, who stayed home to be close to Ned in case he awakened terrified to find himself in a bed still strange to him, and Sam, who couldn't keep his eyes open after nine o'clock, the rest of the family decided to stay up for the midnight service. Kristy, anxious not to miss anything, trailed along, yawning and shivering, half regretting her determination to act grown-up.

The small chapel, hung with swaying brass oil lamps and faded banners, lay at the end of a lane running parallel to the river, at the very edge of the castle park. Village women must have polished the lamps and filled the bowls and baskets with shiny holly and the brave red geraniums Mary had mentioned. Against the brown oak pews and the weathered walls the blossoms shone with neon brightness and made Kristy feel amost cozy as she huddled close to her father's shoulder and waited for the service to begin.

The Hendersons had chosen a back pew, not wishing to intrude on the regular churchgoers, but even so Kristy felt conspicuous in the bright tweed coat she was wearing.

All of the women and girls who passed on their way down the center aisle were dressed in dark clothing, and many of them wore shawls over their heads. Several glanced at the Americans curiously, and sometimes a nod of welcome would be accompanied by a flickering smile, but on the whole the preponderantly female group was sober. The roisterers, Kristy supposed, were in the pubs.

None of the carols were familiar, nor could Kristy understand the minister's dialect when he read the Christmas story. However, she could tell from the prayer book that the service was Episcopalian. She wondered idly whether Fergus O'Malley would be buried from here, or whether the funeral would be held at the big Catholic church with the cross on top, down at the end of the village street.

The mere thought of the unfortunate gardener made Kristy's mind skip backward over the events of the past fourteen hours. It seemed almost impossible that so little time had passed since Sam had discovered the body in the graveyard and given the alarm. Again she pondered the possibility of murder, and wondered how soon the results of the autopsy would be announced. Except for bulk of body and weight of years, Kristy felt like a veritable Miss Marple, caught up in a mystery as intriguing as anyone could wish.

Already she had happened on several clues, clues which seemed significant to her, although she couldn't have said

90

why. As the congregation rose to sing a final hymn, Kristy was recalling the light playing over the shrubbery outside the castle windows the night before. She was thinking of the pages torn from the book entitled *Ghosts in Irish Castles.* She was remembering how she had stood on the tower parapet watching a man drive a panniered donkey down to the river bank, and the signal he had made in response to a whistle from Ballyhooly's grounds.

All these things had happened before Fergus O'Malley's death, but all of them had seemed rather odd to Kristy, and they still did. She wondered, too, why the gardener had been wearing hip boots rather than his ordinary work shoes when he was found.

Somehow she must find out more about this dour man who was now lying in his coffin. Why had his sister-in-law called him stubborn and hard? Why had Liam McMurrough, the coarse-featured fellow in the Fermoy shop, claimed that he was a mean man and a bitter one? Did nobody have a good word to say for Fergus? Even now that he was dead?

There was the soft slap-slap of hymn books shutting, and the congregation remained standing for the Benediction. Then a gust of cold air came rushing through the opened door, and Kristy wound her scarf more tightly around her throat as she reined in her plunging thoughts. At the back of the chapel villagers were gathering around her parents and grandparents, bidding them welcome and

91

remarking that it was sad to have such a blight on the season as Fergus O'Malley's death.

Kristy, standing a little to the rear of the group, sensed people crowding behind her. She glanced over her shoulder and saw a bent old woman clutching a girl's strong arm and pushing ahead blindly. "What's the fuss about, Bridget?" she croaked.

"It's the foreigners at the castle. They've come to service, Mama, and they're talking about dead Fergus O'-Malley, God rest his soul."

"Hmph," muttered the old woman, as Kristy stepped aside to let her pass. "They'll sleep uneasy at the great house tonight, I'll vow. The ghost'll be walkin' and the fish'll be leppin' like always when there's a villain abroad."

"Now, Mama!" the daughter quieted her. "There's no need to talk like that. You know as well as I do that the ghost of Ballyhooly hasn't been abroad since the last big catch."

Any further remarks were drowned in the babble of voices from the doorway. The pair edged past the Hendersons and left the chapel ahead of the group from the castle. They disappeared into the night before Kristy reached the steps, but the daughter's last remark had given her further food for thought. Why did talk of the ghost keep edging into the picture? Who—or what—was the ghost supposed to be?

Not that she was superstitious, Kristy reminded herself

later, as she crawled between linen sheets marvelously warmed by the electric blanket. She was merely curious. From all she could gather, the villagers were talking about the ghost of a fisherman, as indeed the title of the missing chapter about Ballyhooly seemed to indicate.

Instead of lying awake in anticipation of Christmas morning, as she had done for all the years of her childhood, Kristy lay with the covers pulled up around her chin and marveled that her dreaming could take such a strange turn. What would Linda and Beth make of her now, if they could share her thoughts? What would Michael say, if she should tell him that on Christmas morning she had gone to bed wondering how to persuade someone—anyone!—to tell her a ghost story every living soul in each small coteen from Fermoy to Mallow seemed to know?

The castle was quiet, except for the hall clock chiming the small hours of the morning. From the wet stone walls of the tower water dripped silently to the paving stones of the courtyard. Not a creature stirred, not a car passed over the bridge. Even the rooks resting on the ivy-clad walls had stopped twittering and gone to sleep.

As the clock struck three, Kristy's bedroom door creaked with a thin scream as it opened. Suddenly she started bolt upright. There was somebody in her room!

Her heart pounded, her mouth was dry, and terror

93

clutched like a cord around her throat. A hand began to pat at the bedclothes, and she tried to cry out but couldn't utter a sound. The hand touched her arm.

"Hey, Sis!" came Sam's anxious whisper. "There's a light in the tower. Come look!"

"Oh, for Pete's sake!" Kristy flopped back on the warm pillow. "You scared me half to death. Go back to bed! You're imagining things," she scolded.

"I am not!" Sam denied belligerently. "Scaredy-cat! You're afraid to come see for yourself."

This was too much for Kristy. Furious, she leaped out of bed and scurried across the cold floor to the half-open door, edged through it without making it squeak again, and felt her way into Sam's room, where the wan night light from the hall didn't penetrate.

Sam was shivering at her heels. "There!" he whispered. "See!"

7

Sam was right. There was no doubt about it. Narrow slits of light hung in the night like streaks of pale yellow crayon drawn on black paper. They could come from nowhere but the tower windows. The little room offered no other view.

His teeth chattering, Sam leaped under the covers, and Kristy crawled into the warm bed beside him. She pulled the down comforter up around their shoulders as they sat huddled together, staring at the slender beams. Terror and cold were almost equally pitted against each other, and Kristy felt that she could actually hear her heart thumping in her chest.

"We ought to get Mom and Dad," Sam whispered when he could control the clacking of his teeth.

Kristy didn't bother to reply. She lacked the willpower

to budge from this spot. Her knees had turned to jelly and her feet were like ice. "The light's coming from the second floor," she said unnecessarily.

"It's got to be the ghost," her brother muttered under his breath.

"Don't be silly," Kristy advised, but without much conviction, because she was remembering the old village woman's prediction, overheard in the chapel. *"They'll sleep uneasy at the castle . . . the ghost will be walking tonight.* "Don't be silly," Kristy repeated, talking more to herself than to Sam.

"You explain it then."

Kristy couldn't. She knew as well as her brother that Fergus O'Malley had been the keeper of the ancient key to the tower, and this made the ghost theory all too captivating.

The light was moving now, fading away from the window slits, to appear again in an aperture farther down the tower wall. That's the opening on the curve of the stairs, Kristy thought with remarkable clarity, considering her fright. The ghost, or the person—whoever it is—must be coming down to the first floor.

Kristy had an excellent memory. She could picture every detail of the cluttered anteroom, the mildewed garden chairs, the rotting baskets, the rubber boots, the canvas umbrella, and the tattered Maypole leaning crazily in a corner. An insane notion struck her. She could almost hear the Maypole creaking as the ghost skipped around it.

"Ooh!" Sam caught his breath convulsively.

"Sh!" Kristy warned for no reason at all.

Together the pair craned forward, wide-eyed, as the light reappeared once more, raking the time-worn oaken panels on the inside of the tower door. The door must be standing slightly ajar, but not really open, Kristy decided, or the light would have hit the wall and the shrubbery in the courtyard rather than just the face of the dark wood. After another split second the light went out, and the tower was invisible once more.

Sam started to whisper something in Kristy's ear, but she shook her head and cautioned him with a squeeze of his elbow. Listening intently, she could hear muffled footsteps. Then the great door squeaked a brief protest, and a few moments later there was a grating sound, as though a key were turning in the lock.

"That was no ghost," Sam decided aloud after an interval. "That was for real."

"You're getting smart," murmured Kristy, trying to sound self-possessed.

"What could anyone want in the tower at night?"

Kristy shrugged. "Search me."

"And the key," Sam went on. "Where would he get the key?"

"That," Kristy admitted, "is the key question," and

wasn't surprised when her tremulous attempt at humor fell flat.

"It could be Mr. O'Malley's brother, maybe," Sam suggested.

"Even so. . . ."

By the time the clock struck three-thirty they had whispered together for ten minutes more, and Kristy could face the trip back to her own bed. "Now go to sleep, Sam, and stop worrying," she urged. "It's Christmas morning already, and we'll have to get up in a few hours. We don't want to be dead on our feet."

Scampering back to her room, Kristy realized that her metaphor was unfortunate. She was still frightened, more so now without the human comfort of Sam's young body. Deliberately, she left both bedroom doors ajar, and crept under the electric blanket to lie shivering for half an hour before she finally fell asleep.

The next time she opened her eyes, Kristy found her mother smiling down at her in the dimness that passed for daylight in an Irish December. "Good morning, darling, and Merry Christmas! Do you know what time it is? Nearly nine o'clock."

Kristy stretched and yawned, smiling back at her mother as she raised herself on her elbows. She grew sober as the night's strange episode flashed back into her consciousness. "Is Sam awake yet?" she asked.

"No, and I can't understand it. He's usually up before

98

anyone else in the house. On Christmas morning especially."

Kristy could explain the situation and did, as quickly as possible. "You'd better talk to Sam if you don't want him to get Grandma upset," she said. "He'll be full of the story, and whether anybody believes him or not, opening Christmas presents will seem like—" She stopped, searching for a word.

"Like an anticlimax," her mother put in. "I'll go speak to him now," she promised. At the door, however, she turned and frowned. "You're sure, Kristy, that you weren't imagining things. That it wasn't a street light, or perhaps a lamp shining from Nora's room downstairs?"

Kristy shook her head vigorously. "You know I don't make things up. I used to, maybe, when I was Sam's age, but I always admitted I was fibbing, later on."

"Well, get up and get dressed," her mother said with a sigh. "I know it will be difficult, but we must all try not to alarm your grandparents. Fergus O'Malley's death was bad enough, but if they get the feeling we have prowlers on the grounds, they'll wish they'd never leased this place at all."

What her mother said or did to keep Sam quiet Kristy couldn't imagine. Breakfast passed peacefully, and the opening of the token gifts scattered under the Christmas tree was fun. There were miniature games and puzzles, books for the grown-ups, and playthings for Ned, who

99

shouted in delight at each package he was handed and insisted on unwrapping his presents all by himself.

By midmorning the last thank you was said, the last paper burned in the fireplace, and the sun, emerging from the clouds above the Nagles Mountains, was routing the hoarfrost that had dusted the countryside with white.

To Kristy's informed eye, her brother was beginning to look like the cat who swallowed the canary. He was bursting with information, and could scarcely keep from disgorging the news about the ghostly visitor to the tower.

"Wouldn't this be a good time to take the presents down to the O'Malley children?" his mother proposed cleverly. "Why don't you and Kristy go to the cottage together, and while you're there ask Mrs. O'Malley if there's anything further we can do."

Kristy was more than willing to act as emissary. She gathered up the heap of small packages wrapped the night before, and led Sam quickly to the park gate, where a cattle guard was stretched across a deep ditch, and a gravel path jutted off at an angle toward the square little house usually occupied by Ballyhooly's gardener. At the O'Malley cottage, smoke was curling from a central chimney, and a calico cat played on the doorstep, pushing a candy wrapper about with sheathed paws. Even before Kristy knocked, the door burst open. Patrick O'Malley, a ruddy, clean-shaven man in a fresh white shirt and a thick sweater cried, "Come in, come in. And a Merry Christmas to ye!" A stranger to the situation might have thought there had been no death in the family at all.

Kristy introduced herself and her brother, and Mr. O'Malley shook hands heartily with each of them. "It's very kind you've been to my childer," he said appreciatively, and shouted for his wife, who appeared in the doorway with Dagan, Ormond, Brian, and Breeda surrounding her like a brood of chicks. Only Rosaleen hung back, conscious of her seniority, and looked from Kristy to Sam with shy delight.

"We've brought some little things for the children, the kind we call stocking presents in the United States," said Kristy rather grandly. Basking in Rosaleen's admiring gaze, she couldn't help playing the lady from the castle.

Sam was embarrassed by the performance. He snatched one of the presents from her hands, read the tag and thrust the parcel at Ormond, saying gruffly, "Here," while he kept his eyes on the floor.

Ormond's "Thank you" was almost inaudible, and the rest of the children seemed equally overwhelmed, but Kristy was sure they were pleased. They turned the red-tissue-wrapped packages in their small chapped hands and stared down at them, although to open them in the presence of Kristy and Sam was apparently a feat they dared not attempt.

The visit, therefore, was a short one. Mrs. O'Malley passed around chocolate candies, which she called sweets, and Mr. O'Malley made a short speech about appreciating the Hendersons' thoughtfulness. But to Kristy's disappointment not a word was said concerning the tragedy of the day before. In fact, the parents of the five Irish children seemed fully as anxious as Kristy's grandmother to maintain the illusion that this Christmas could be a merry one, with everyone smiling and full of normal holiday cheer.

Patrick O'Malley seemed to Kristy as engaging as his brother had been glum. He followed the Hendersons out to the steps and waved them off, shouting to call on him "for anything at all, if need be." If he was grieved by the death of Fergus, he concealed his sorrow well, and acted like any other family man on a Christmas morning, cordial and at ease.

Sam ran ahead along the drive to meet Uncle Robert and Aunt Irene, who were coming from the castle with Ned between them. The child let go of his parents' hands and galloped toward Sam, calling his name like a cheer.

"He's voted you Man of the Year," Uncle Robert said with a grin.

Since Sam didn't catch the allusion, his aunt added, speaking to Kristy, "Ned thinks Sam is the best Christmas present of all. It must be fun to discover a boy cousin all of a sudden, especially one who's practically grown up."

Flattered, Sam allowed Ned to grab his hand with a mittened paw and drag him back toward the gate. "We're

102

going for a walk," Uncle Robert explained. "The others will be along in a minute. They'll meet us on the bridge."

"*Sur le pont d'Avignon, on y danse, on y danse,*" Aunt Irene began to sing, and Ned, surprisingly, started to sing along too, in French baby talk.

"He'll sing in French, but he won't talk French," Uncle Robert said to Kristy in an undertone as they came along behind. "He understands the language well enough, but he'll answer a French question in English every time."

The road beyond the castle walls curved sharply downhill, and although there was no traffic, everyone kept well to the side, kicking up the half-frozen leaves with the toes of their boots. They passed a rusted gate set in the stone, an outside entrance that gave on the neglected graveyard where Fergus had been found. Skidding and slipping on the wet weeds and grass, Kristy climbed the bank and peered through the grille, but all she could see were leaning slabs of mildewed marble thrusting up through the undergrowth.

The bridge, old and worn by American standards, arched gracefully over the steel-colored river, beyond which a low yellow building crouched under a thatched roof. Before it hung a sign shaped like a fish, bearing letters that Kristy could read, even from a distance. "The Wily Salmon," she said. "Do you suppose that's another pub?"

103

The question was rhetorical, and she wasn't surprised when nobody answered. Her aunt had opened a sketchbook and in spite of the cold was making a quick drawing of the winding river, while her uncle was waving a greeting to the rest of the family, who came straggling down the road in ones and twos. Sam lifted Ned in his arms to give him a glimpse of the water below the bridge. "Hold him there!" shouted Grandpa, hurrying ahead with a camera banging against his chest. "I want to get your picture!"

Everyone had to pose for him, in groups and individually. He ran boyishly from one side of the bridge to the other, finding the best angles, the best light. Then he left the road and followed a path along the far bank, focusing again and again on the castle, as it rose, tall and stately, above its terraced gardens and the meadows at the riverside.

Kristy wandered after him, stepping gingerly along the muddy track, beside which dead ferns rattled in the winter air. Hands dug into her coat pockets, toes curling frigidly inside her high winter boots, she was tired of sauntering along with the others, who were suiting their pace to Ned's.

Grandpa was glad of her company. "Come on," he suggested. "Let's really step out and see where this cow path leads. Otherwise we'll freeze to death."

Kristy hesitated, then decided that a little more mud

on her boots wouldn't matter, and tucked her hand through her grandfather's arm. They walked along as briskly as possible, sometimes on stretches of short, tufted grass, but often on a bridlepath marked by the hooves of sheep and cows as well as horses. The prints were crusted with ice, but at every second step Kristy's feet sank into the mud. Her grandfather was now marching ahead, and they proceeded single file around a bend in the Blackwater until they were opposite the castle's boathouse, the windows of which wore a hooded look, like half-shut eyes.

"Have I told you about the present owner of the castle?" Grandpa called over his shoulder. "He's a Britisher —a sporting man. Comes here for the fishing once a year, but rents the big house to people like us the rest of the time."

"Daddy wants to go fishing, as soon as the season opens," Kristy called back.

"And so he shall, if we can find him a gillie," her grandfather answered. He crossed a stile at the edge of a field and turned to give her a hand over. "Warming up?" he asked.

Kristy nodded, untruthfully.

"So am I. Shall we go on a little farther, then?"

For five minutes they walked on, the castle now out of sight. They crossed a rickety trestle over a muddy ditch, then struck a dry patch of path leading through a grove of trees.

This, Kristy recognized, must be the copse toward which the donkey driver had turned yesterday morning. Visible from the tower parapet, but not from the castle, it was the only sizeable grove along this bank. She glanced around curiously, but found nothing of special interest. The whistled signal from the castle grounds that she had heard the day before yesterday was still inexplicable, and probably not worth pondering over.

Grandpa had paused at the edge of the trees ahead to watch a farmer lead a red Kerry bull toward a fenced field. The path skirted the field, then wound down a muddy slope to the riverbank, and stopped at the verge of a long, narrow belt of bog, black as the birds wheeling above it. The river was sluggish here, and shallow pools of slimy water winked back at the sky. On the opposite bank, where a row of wispy trees hung over the stream, a great gray-blue heron, still as a statue, stood on a fallen log.

"Look, Grandpa!" Kristy whispered, spotting the bird first.

The camera came up, the shutter clicked, and at the unfamiliar sound the bird came alive, skimming over the flat water in a flopping flight. Its wings seemed to move in slow motion as it rose. Gaining height in a succession of mounting curves, it gleamed against the sky, then vanished over the copse of trees.

"Beautiful!" Kristy breathed.

Her grandfather agreed. Then his glance dropped to

106

the river at their feet. "Not so beautiful," he said, pointing to a hideous fish nearly two feet long lying close to the surface of a layer of scum. One side of the face was scarred by a white film , and near the feebly moving tail a gray veil covered the black scales.

Kristy shuddered. "What is it?"

"A salmon, nearly dead. He's made it upstream this far, heaven knows how, but he's almost done for, poor fellow. There's some sort of disease that has been hitting the salmon in the Blackwater, according to the Cork *Examiner*. Nobody seems to know what's causing it, but it could be factory waste from up around Mallow. Look at the debris in that eddy and the foam on top."

Kristy looked, although she found the sight distasteful. Her skin prickled at the sight of the struggling fish, and she quickly turned away.

"Never heard of ecology, these country folk," her grandfather muttered to himself. "Great pity."

The words were lost on Kristy. She was looking down at the half-frozen mud at her feet, marked by a long indentation that ran straight to the water, the sort of mark that could have been made by the keel of a small boat. Then, as her eyes flicked back toward the grove of trees, she gave a sudden gasp and started to scramble up the bank. A patch of brown, almost indistinguishable from the fallen leaves, had caught her attention.

A moment later she reached the spot and bent quickly

to pick up a woolen cap. Holding it out gingerly, she cried, "Look, Grandpa! Could this be the cap that Fergus used to wear?"

"It certainly looks like it." Kristy's grandfather took the cap from her and turned it in his hands. "We'll take it along to Mrs. O'Malley, shall we? Certainly she should recognize it."

"But what would he be doing on this side of the river?" Kristy asked, not because she was expecting a logical answer. She was merely thinking out loud, remembering the donkey driver glimpsed from the tower, and the whistle that might have come from Fergus himself. What appointment could have been so secret that it would have brought him across the river in a boat? On an impulse she told her grandfather what she had seen, then said, "Finding the cap may be very important, because it means there's a real connection between the two men, wouldn't you say?"

"It's possible," her grandfather agreed. "Even probable." He rolled the cap in a cone and stuffed it into his coat pocket, then examined the frozen ground more carefully. "Looks like the mark of a boat's keel, all right."

"Wait till we tell the others!" cried Kristy excitedly. "It could be our first real clue!"

"Now wait a minute!" Grandpa demurred. "No talk of Fergus is going to spoil your grandmother's Christmas day. It'll be time enough to take the cap to Mrs. O'Malley tomorrow. And in the meantime it's doing no harm resting right here in my pocket. Let's keep it a secret between us, Kristy. Shake hands on it. What do you say?"

Kristy shook hands reluctantly, unable to conceal her disappointment. Much as she adored her grandfather she couldn't help but wish he were more venturesome. How could he just pocket the cap and keep quiet for the rest of this livelong day?

He seemed to understand her dismay better than she expected. "Tell you what," he said as they started back to the castle. "You found the cap, so you should be the one to take it to Mrs. O'Malley and see if she recognizes it. I'll tuck it away in the bottom drawer of my bureau, and you can get it from there any time tomorrow you like."

8

The day after Christmas is Saint Stephen's Day in Ireland. Since this year it fell on a Saturday, the people celebrated it by shutting down all stores and business establishments and claiming an extra holiday. Horse races were held in Limerick and Dublin. Vans carried the mounts of the local gentry to the starting points of half a hundred fox hunts. Laborers, relishing the time off from work, gathered in pubs, and through every village and town in Ireland the Wren Boys trooped, begging for alms.

Kristy couldn't believe her eyes when she came on a pair capering up the drive toward the castle. They were tall fellows, young men almost, dressed as though they were off to a Halloween party, their faces blackened with charcoal, their costumes made from bits and pieces of bright cloth.

She backed away, frightened at first, because the boys laughed and teased her. Then her grandfather appeared in the castle doorway, ready to come to her rescue. At once the lads took off their carnival hats, made a deep bow, and burst into song.

The wren, the wren, the King of all birds,
　Saint Stephen's Day was caught in the furze.
Although he is little his family is great.
　Cheer up, dear landlord, and give us a treat!

Nora appeared with some slices of Mrs. Quinn's Christmas cake, and Grandpa dug in his pockets and came up with some shillings and sixpence. The boys accepted the gifts politely, with grins of appreciation, while Kristy stood by marveling that customs in their two countries should be so different in timing, yet so alike in performance.

"Trick or treat, the day after Christmas," she murmured when the Wren Boys were out of earshot. "You never can tell what the Irish will dream up next."

Running upstairs from the kitchen with a picnic basket on her arm, Aunt Irene called, "We're going to drive to Limerick to the races, Kristy. There's an extra seat in the car. Want to come along?"

"Who's going?" Kristy asked.

111

"Your Uncle Robert, your grandmother, and I. Mary is going to take care of Ned while we're away."

"How long a drive is it?"

"About an hour and a quarter each way."

"I think I'll stay here," Kristy decided. The memory of the long and tedious drive from Dublin had not yet faded. She was tired of jouncing about in the back seat of a little car. Besides, she had an important errand to do.

"Let me go!" Sam begged, appearing from nowhere, but his grandfather shook his head. "You're too young, Sambo. Besides, I've changed my mind after seeing that picnic basket. I think I'll go along myself."

The Limerick party got off in a flurry. Frosty car windows had to be wiped clean, binoculars found, gloves and scarves and car rugs collected, and at the last minute Aunt Irene had run back to the house for her sketchbook. But at last everyone was ready. Only Ned, kept below stairs by Mary, failed to wave good-bye. Immediately afterward, Sam and his father went off to explore Cregg Castle, a ruin they had spotted from the road to Fermoy, while Kristy and her mother went into the warm drawing room, ostensibly to write postcards and to read.

Within half an hour Kristy, increasingly restless, decided to walk into the village to mail her completed cards. "The post office won't be open," her mother warned her, but she went off nevertheless, after taking the brown cap from her grandfather's bureau drawer and stuffing it in her shoulder bag.

The O'Malley's house was curtained and quiet this morning. Nobody answered Kristy's knock, although in the side yard a line of washing flapped stiffly in the freezing breeze. If the funeral is planned for today, Kristy thought, the Wren Boys roaming the village streets will lend a bizarre note to the proceedings. It seemed likely, although she wasn't sure what was customary, that the burial would be put off for another day.

Across the road from the castle gate a painted gypsy wagon was drawn up on a square of level ground. The shafts were empty; a horse, skinny but strong-looking, was tethered to a nearby tree. To the rear of the cleared space a bearded man had set up a temporary shop, and was tinkering with a broken kitchen utensil while a village woman stood by, watching and waiting. A dark-skinned toddler played with a puppy under the wagon wheels, while his black-haired gypsy mother was shaking out a quilt beside the van.

The minute she saw Kristy approaching the road the woman came hurrying over. "Your fortune, beautiful missy? Three questions answered, the future told, all for a ten shilling note."

"That's too much!" said Kristy, feigning shock, although gypsy fortune-tellers around Dublin always tried for a pound.

The woman shrugged, and glanced over Kristy's shoulder at the castle rising beyond the trees of the park. "You're American," she said, recognizing the accent.

Then she added in a wheedling tone, "Americans are always rich."

"*I'm* not," Kristy protested, although she was feeling comparatively wealthy this morning. A fortnight's unspent allowance was in her pocket, and the opportunity of having her fortune told was tempting. She knew precisely what questions she would ask.

The baby crawled out from beneath the wagon and went to his mother, where he clung to her long, full skirt. "A crust of bread for the little one," the woman coaxed, catching the child up and cradling him against her bosom. "You are a pretty girl, missy, very pretty. You will have many admirers, I foresee. That and much more I can predict." The gypsy was obviously well-spoken.

Bargaining, Kristy said, "I'll give you six shillings if you'll answer two questions." Her eyes twinkled mischievously.

"Eight," the gypsy countered.

Kristy was ready to give in. The sum was less than an American dollar, and she had questions to which she truly needed answers. One thing she must make sure of, however. "Do you come from around here?" she asked.

The woman hesitated, appearing to ponder the answer that would be most acceptable. "We travel only County Cork," she said finally, and looked relieved when Kristy smiled. "Come sit down." Setting the baby on the ground, the mother sent him scampering. "I have two stools."

114

She brought them out and set them between the wagon shafts, so that any passerby could see she was doing business. As she moved about she continued to flatter Kristy, commenting on her warm clothes, her lovely hair, her good fortune at being in Ireland at Christmastime. Her eyes were shrewd, and her voice was deep and cajoling, with a touch of refinement about it at odds with her tawdry earrings and her ragged skirt.

"First, let me see your palm," the gypsy said, after Kristy had handed over four two-shilling pieces. "Ah, a fine straight lifeline, and a happy marriage. An early one, too. You are a lucky girl!"

Marriage was not a subject in which Kristy was immediately interested, although it was pleasant to learn that she might expect four children, that her husband would be handsome, and that she would see many foreign places before she died.

Finally the time came for her two questions. "Do you know the story of the ghost of Ballyhooly?" Kristy asked.

The fortune-teller threw back her head and laughed spontaneously. "Sure, and everybody around here knows that old story, for what it's worth."

"Tell it to me, then."

The gypsy was willing enough. "In Ireland ghosts appear only in houses that have known true happiness or true misery," she said. "Up until the time I was your age Ballyhooly Castle was known as a happy house. Lady Listowell had lived to a great age, and the tribulations of the Roche were long forgotten. Then it was sold to an Englishman, who began to come regularly for the fishing. That's when the trouble began."

"What trouble?" Kristy asked.

"Why, the trouble with the fish, of course," said the fortune-teller in a surprised tone. "You must have heard about the ghostly catch."

Kristy shook her head, not trusting herself to speak. She was too excited by the prospect of at last hearing the story missing from the book.

The gypsy settled back on her stool. "I'm not sure of the year," she said, "but there was a time when the salmon churned up the Blackwater like demons, leaping the weirs at Fermoy and plunging right past Castle Hyde, Cregg Castle, and Ballyhooly itself. The folks who saw them say they were as thick as sardines in a can. Giant fish, strong and determined, healthy as my baby here, and twice as plump. Fishermen couldn't throw in a line, lest it get tangled among the scales and fins grinding together, they were that thick. All headed for Mallow and beyond." She paused and spread her hands. "That was one day."

"And the next?" Kristy prompted.

"The next it was all over. Less than a mile beyond the castle here the salmon began to leap high out of the water and dart around crazily. Then suddenly all the fish gave up, just stopped fighting. The people who saw the scene can't explain it, but anyone could pick the salmon right

116

out of the water. They were done for. Done *in*, some say, by the ghost of Ballyhooly. Because it was just at the edge of the Ballyhooly waters that they sickened and began to float back downstream.

"Now comes the really terrible part." With the concentration of a born storyteller, the gypsy leaned forward, resting her elbows on her knees and clasping her hands as she looked into Kristy's face. "Just short of the bridge at Fermoy the dead fish began to pile up, millions of them, until a person could walk across the river on their backs. The ravens and the rooks settled over them like a black blanket, but even the birds wouldn't touch their flesh."

"Were they poisoned?" Kristy asked.

The gypsy nodded solemnly. "By a spell cast from that tower, like as not."

"But why?"

"Ghosts in Irish castles don't need a reason," the fortune-teller muttered grumpily. "But I can tell you one thing. Every tenth year since that time there's been a strange death at the castle, just before the salmon begin leaping upstream."

"Like Fergus O'Malley?" breathed Kristy, certain that the gypsies must have heard about the gardener.

The woman shook her head. "Before this," she said, "it has always been a foreign landlord or one of his guests who have died, and Ballyhooly folk say that

117

each time a person perishes on the castle grounds the ghost walks in the tower that same night."

Kristy shivered. Forgetting that she was still owed the answer to a second question, she thanked the fortune-teller with as much politeness as she could muster and wandered off toward the post office with the absorbed look of a reader in the midst of a compelling novel. She'd heard the eerie tale of the ghost of Ballyhooly at last.

As her mother had predicted, the post office was indeed closed, but in the street outside the pubs sidewalks were being swept, and from the direction of the church came the entire O'Malley family, seven strong.

Kristy felt it would be rude to accost them on the street, but she trailed them home, and at the front door of the cottage pulled out the brown cap and told Mrs. O'Malley the circumstances of finding it. "Do you think it belonged to Fergus?" she asked.

"Without a question of a doubt," replied Mrs. O'Malley. "Come in, Miss Kristy, come in. Himself gave it to his brother for Christmas a year ago. See, here's the label of the Fermoy store where it was bought. Look, Patrick!" she called. "Look what Mr. Henderson and this young lady found!"

Mr. O'Malley was quick to corroborate his wife's declaration that the cap had indeed belonged to Fergus. "Where did you come across it? Down by the boathouse? That would figure."

118

Kristy shook her head. "On the opposite bank of the river, up a bit from the castle grounds, near that copse of trees that come right down to the water's edge."

"Did you now?" Mr. O'Malley looked puzzled. "What could Fergus have been doing over there at this time of year. That's a very strange thing, sure enough."

The children, meanwhile, had gathered around, the older ones listening curiously, the younger three gazing at Kristy with large, admiring eyes. They were getting more accustomed to the presence of the American young people and weren't nearly as timid as they had been a few days before.

In fact, Rosaleen gathered courage to ask Kristy to take off her coat and stay awhile, looking so eager that it was impossible to refuse. Copying Kristy's action on the day before Christmas, she took her into a small bedroom and presented her few small treasures for inspection—a locket with a faded picture of her mother as a girl, a doll in a Spanish costume, an enameled pin shaped like a ship.

"Aren't you lucky to have a room of your own!" exclaimed Kristy after being duly appreciative. In such a small house she had expected the children to be crowded together in a single bedchamber.

"I just moved in here this morning," confessed

Rosaleen. "It used to be where my Uncle Fergus slept."

"Goodness, don't you mind?" Kristy's question burst forth spontaneously; then she bit her lip and wondered how she could apologize.

Rosaleen, however, was quite unabashed. "I like it," she said cheerfully. "It's lovely to be alone."

Of course it would be lovely to be alone, Kristy thought, distressed by her lack of perception. Having never shared a bedroom with anyone, she could only surmise what privacy could mean to this young girl who would soon become teen-age. Apparently Rosaleen didn't have a qualm about the previous occupant. This room was hers now—hers alone—and she was showing it off with shy pride.

Kristy got up and began to prowl around, looking out the window hung with starched white curtains, touching a chair arm, the side of the worn deal bureau, glancing at Rosaleen's reflection in the mirror, then down at a wastebasket her toe had inadvertantly bumped.

Rosaleen jumped up from the bed. "Oh, I meant to empty that," she said, but Kristy scarcely heard. She was stooping to pick up a sheaf of folded paper, cream-colored printed pages that had been torn carefully from a book. At the top was a running legend, clearly visible: "Ballyhooly's Ghostly Catch."

"Where did you find this, Rosaleen? It's a chapter missing from a book up at the castle."

120

Rosaleen immediately looked frightened. She stood with her hands clasped behind her back and said, "I didn't take it, honestly. It was in the drawer of the table by the bed. It must have been something Uncle Fergus had."

"Of course," Kristy agreed, keeping her voice level and making every effort to be casual. She riffled the several pages and said calmly, "It's a story I've been wanting to read. Do you mind if I take it along?"

Relieved, Rosaleen began to smile again. "Of course not," she said. "Maybe you could paste it back in the book."

A few minutes later Kristy took her leave, the missing story in her hands at last. She burst in upon her mother, waving the pages triumphantly, "Look what Rosaleen found in Fergus O'Malley's room!"

Valerie Henderson was engaged in the process of starting to knit a sweater, using several of the more complicated Aran Island stitches. She had the instruction book open on her lap, and was frowning down at it in concentration.

"What's that, dear?" she asked.

"The story missing from the ghost book on Irish castles. *You* know."

"Oh, yes."

Kristy, without bothering to take off her coat, had

121

flopped down in a chair. "Don't you want me to read it to you?"

"Could we make it a little later, Kristy? After I've done just three more rows?"

"I guess." Kristy smoothed out the folded pages and read the story to herself, skimming from one paragraph to the next with a growing feeling of deflation. The tale was substantially the same as that told by the gypsy fortune-teller, embroidered here and there with long passages of descriptions, but offering no new facts.

"Oh, pooh," she complained as she neared the end. "There's nothing new in here, nothing at all. The only curious thing is why Fergus O'Malley should have had it tucked away in his table drawer."

"Yes, that is rather odd," her mother agreed absently. She was still absorbed in the knitting directions and spoke without emphasis.

Kristy sighed, got up and shrugged out of her coat, then hunted up *Ghosts in Irish Castles*, which had been left under a stack of books on top of the drawing room bookcase. "Do we have any scotch tape?" she asked.

"I don't think so, but you can get some in the village tomorrow."

Kristy slipped the story into the proper place and put the book back on the shelf. She wished her mother would be more companionable, but it was hopeless to try to interrupt her when she was so engrossed.

122

It wasn't until teatime, actually, when the entire family was once more gathered around the peat fire in the drawing room, that Kristy had a chance to tell the story of Ballyhooly's Ghostly Catch, and then it was the gypsy's version that she repeated, because it was so much shorter and more dramatic than the account in the book.

She began chronologically, braving the certain criticism she knew would come.

"I've told you not to go hobnobbing with gypsies, Kristy. Some of them can be downright dangerous," her mother said.

"I don't think this one was dangerous," Kristy argued. "She was a little greedy, but she was sort of nice."

"And her husband is a tinker who works at his trade," put in Kristy's father. "Sam and I stopped and watched him for a bit, on our way back from Castle Cregg."

"Anyway," said Grandma, "let the child tell her story."

Kristy tried to remember the fortune-teller's exact words, although some of the colorful phrasing escaped her.

Aunt Irene was the most impressed. "That's very interesting, Kristy," she said. "Very interesting indeed. At the back of these old ghost stories there is generally

123

a kernel of truth. I wouldn't be surprised if something like that fish story actually happened."

Stephen Henderson's eyes twinkled with a professional glint. "Any day of your life in Ireland," he said, " 'you may see in haunted Connaught, a dead king walk.' "

"What's that got to do with the price of eggs?" inquired Sam, baffled by the quotation.

"Not very much," said Aunt Irene, her eyes twinkling. "Mathematicians have no imagination, none at all."

"You read too many mysteries, Irene" Kristy's father countered. He stretched his long legs, got up and walked over to the bookshelves, seeking out the shabby, leather-bound book on the fishing rivers of Ireland. As he carried it back to his chair, he said, "This man Augustus Trimble has some interesting facts—and I stress the word *facts*, Irene!—about the Blackwater. For one thing, before 1862 no salmon could get above King's Gap in Lismore Weir. That's near the Duke of Devonshire's big castle, twenty miles or so below Fermoy."

Sam picked up a map from the table at his elbow, unfolded it and sat staring at it aimlessly, having lost interest in the conversation. Kristy was about to break in. She wanted to tell everyone about finding the lost pages from the ghost book, but her father was speaking again, apparently in order to make some sort of point.

"Back in those days," he said, "most of the salmon were caught in the lower reaches of the river with snap

124

nets, or in the fifteen-mile-long estuary by drift nets set by poachers. In some years, the catch was tremendous— up to three hundred thousand fish—yet the owners of riparian rights above Fermoy saw scarcely a grilse in the open season. They just weren't getting up this far."

"What's a grilse?" asked Sam curiously.

"An adolescent salmon, son. One that has spent a year in the ocean. I hope I can show you some before we leave here. They're streamlined and graceful, sharp-nosed and small, with a discernible fork in their tails."

Irene grinned at her brother. "You always wax poetic about fishing, Steve. It's the only time you step out of character."

"Not true!" countered Kristy's mother defensively. "Stephen has as many quotations on the tip of his tongue as Grandpa. I don't know when he finds the time to memorize so much."

"It's not a matter of memorizing. It's a matter of having a good memory. We're not all so fortunate," said Grandma.

"To continue," said Kristy's father, turning the pages of the book, "Mr. Trimble says that by the turn of the century the Blackwater and its tributaries were over-poached. Caretakers were powerless to stop the villains responsible, and feared for their lives. Then came a time of reform, when new laws were passed and fishing with nets was forbidden. That's when sport fishermen began to

125

flock to this part of the country, and some of the big houses were bought up by English and Americans."

"Then it's perfectly possible that all of a sudden millions of salmon could have made it up the river this far?" Kristy questioned.

"Well, let's say thousands, to be on the safe side," her father suggested with a smile.

"And allow for an Irishman's normal tendency to exaggerate," added Grandpa, his eyes twinkling.

"But the story *could* be true, mostly," Kristy persisted.

"It could be true, partly," replied her father. "To that I'll agree."

This was a minor victory, Kristy felt, but a victory nevertheless. "Do you believe the fish all died suddenly, and were swept downstream?" she asked her father.

"I won't say I believe it, but I'll admit it's a possibility. Something could have poisoned them."

"What?" asked Sam unexpectedly.

"There's a big flap about pollution in the newspapers," put in Uncle Robert, who had been poking up the fire at intervals but hadn't entered the discussion so far.

"That's now, not then, dear," Aunt Irene said gently.

At that moment Nora appeared in the doorway and spoke to Grandma Henderson. "I've come to ask permission, madam, for the three of us—Mrs. Quinn and Mary and myself—to take two hours off in the middle of the

126

morning tomorrow. We'd like to go to Fergus O'Malley's funeral, if you can spare us the time."

This ended all talk of ghost stories and fishing. After Grandma had said, "But of course, Nora," and the maid had departed, all of the adults conferred in low voices about the role the "Yanks from the castle" should assume.

"Should we go to the services or stay away?" Aunt Irene asked.

"Wouldn't we feel like intruders?" Kristy's mother wondered aloud.

"I think it depends on what Mr. and Mrs. O'Malley would like us to do," said Grandpa. To Kristy this sounded eminently sensible.

Unexpectedly, Grandma spoke up. "We're none of us going, and that's that. I'll not have our holiday ruined by Fergus O'Malley's misfortune. We only laid eyes on the man twice, while he was alive."

Her decisiveness broke the tension that had crept into the group. Stephen Henderson chuckled. "You tell 'em, Mother!" he teased.

Bringing her chin up defensively, Kristy's grandmother allowed herself a second assertion of authority. "I don't care," she said, "I'm your hostess, so it's up to all of you to do as I see fit."

The decision was a real disappointment for Kristy, although she knew better than to argue. What further clues to the mystery of the gardener's death she had hoped to pick up at the funeral she couldn't have said, but there was always the chance that an overheard remark or an unexpected happening might add another plum to the pudding of the thickening plot.

9

Kristy respected her grandmother's command to stay away from the church where the services were held, but not a word had been said about watching the funeral cortege make its way to the cemetery. To contrive to be in the village when the procession went past was as easy as pie.

Sneaking off from Sam, who was fortunately engrossed in pasting Irish mementos in a Christmas scrapbook, Kristy bought some scotch tape at Sullivan's general store and loitered there, looking at the heterogeneous merchandise in the showcases, until the rattle of wagon wheels and clip-clop of horses' hooves brought her to the door.

She stepped outside and stood pressed against the building, trying to be as inconspicuous as possible. Opposite, in the post-office entrance, an old man stood enjoying the peaty smoke of a black cobeen. "Sure, now, and that'll be Fergus O'Malley on his last trip," she heard him call to someone inside. Then he took off his cap and added as an afterthought, "God rest his soul."

The hearse, a small, closed wagon, was afloat with black funeral plumes, waving like beach grass blowing in a freshening breeze. The sun had appeared, lighting the bleak street and touching the rim of the distant, blue-violet mountains like the edge of a dream.

Behind the hearse walked Mr. and Mrs. Patrick O'Malley, both clad in black. Neither of them spotted Kristy, because at the moment they passed the store they began chatting brightly with friends. Instead of being shocked, as she might have been before she came to live in Ireland, Kristy knew that few of the mourners were likely to make a conventional show of grief. As her father had told her when they had come upon a similar funeral procession in Dublin, "Life is hard here, and the afterlife is very real and not to be feared."

Walking sedately behind the O'Malleys came all of the Ballyhooly villagers who could be spared from their jobs. Behind the three women who worked at the castle came other people who presumably had been friends of the dead man. Among the stragglers was a bearded face that Kristy recognized as Liam McMurrough's, encountered when she was buying paper and ribbon in the Fermoy shop. What had he called Fergus O'Malley? A mean man and a bitter one, or something of the sort. If there had been no love lost between the two, why was McMurrough here, stringing along with the rest?

At the very end of the line, and slightly apart from it, vehicles held up by the funeral procession inched along. There was a cart piled high with peat, a milk truck, and on its far side a young man on a bicycle, who had slowed down too much to maintain his balance. As he edged off the seat and began to walk the bike slowly along, Kristy started forward.

"Michael!" she cried.

"Ah, Kristy! I stopped at the castle, and they told me I might find you along here." Michael leaned the bicycle negligently against the store front, pulled off the knitted cap he was wearing, and grasped Kristy's hands. His eyes were merry as he held her off and grinned appreciatively. "I've been missing you," he said.

"How did you get here, Michael?" gasped Kristy, then remembered. "You're visiting your aunt in Fermoy?"

Michael nodded. "Hitched a ride from Dublin with a chap who was going to Cork," he said as though he had been very clever. "Aunt Sheila was even more surprised to see me than you are."

"She couldn't have been," breathed Kristy. "I'm so surprised I'm practically speechless." Then she recovered herself. "Oh, Michael, I've needed somebody to talk to! I'm so glad you're here."

"You mean there's nine of you at the castle and you haven't a soul to talk to?" Michael asked with a chuckle.

"You know what I mean. Nobody my own age."

"I'm not your age. I'm two years older!"

"Oh, Michael, please don't tease." Pulling her coat collar up around her neck, Kristy was aware of how cold she had grown, standing here. "Let's go back to the castle or somewhere—anywhere—to get warm."

"The pubs will be opening in a minute or two," Michael suggested. "Come on across the street and I'll buy you an orange squash or a cup of tea."

When she had first come to Ireland such a proposal would have seemed brash to Kristy, but she had long since learned that even young children sometimes went to pubs with their parents. Irish pubs were more like coffeehouses than saloons. They were gathering places where a woman frequently tended bar, and where a sixteen-year-old girl need not feel out of place.

"All right," Kristy agreed, "but make it a *pot* of tea. Whoever said the south of Ireland has a mild, semitropical climate was dead wrong."

"There are palm trees growing within five miles of Fermoy," Michael said. "I've seen them."

"And I've seen hoarfrost so thick it looks like icing on a cake," Kristy said. "I wouldn't be surprised to see snow."

The door to the pub was opened precisely on time by a young boy with a broom in his hand. "Come along in,"

132

he said. "There's a fire started inside." With a jerk of his head he indicated a small sitting room next to the main one half filled by a high bar of scarred brown wood.

Kristy and Sam went at once to the fireplace, where they rubbed their hands and held them out toward the feeble flame. "You'll have to wait a bit to be served," the boy said, "but you can make yourselves at home."

"Where is everybody?" Michael asked.

"To the funeral," said the boy. "Where else? They'll be back in a few minutes, though. On a cold day like this they won't linger." As he started to sweep the worn floorboards in the barroom, dust rose around his legs like fog, and into the small room he eventually swept a black and white cat, who mewed a complaint, then came and rubbed against Kristy's legs.

Michael drew two straight chairs as close to the fire as he dared. "We may as well sit down while we're waiting," he suggested sensibly.

Kristy unwound her scarf and unbuttoned her coat. She was beginning to warm up a little. "How long can you stay?" she asked. "Will you come to the castle for lunch?"

Michael accepted at once. "I was hoping you'd ask me." He glanced around the walls of the shabby room, where flyspecked World War II posters, brown and crackling with age, hung against distempered paper. Above the hearth was an oil painting of Ballyhooly Castle, carefully detailed but obviously the work of an amateur. The tower

133

rose against a murky sky, and the water of the river looked solid enough to skate across. "Tell me about your Christmas, Kristy. Was it fun?" Michael asked, returning his attention to his companion.

"Under the circumstances, yes," Kristy said.

"Under what circumstances?"

"Well, you see, the gardener died—or was killed—the day before Christmas. That was his funeral you were following. It was all pretty grim, because Sam and my aunt and I found him, lying dead in the castle graveyard, and nobody seems to be sure whether it was an accident or a murder, but they've done an autopsy and the police have been around asking us questions and—"

"Whoa! Slow down, Kristy. Start over. This sounds very upsetting—and sad."

"Oh, it is, Michael. And mysterious. Because the castle is supposed to be haunted, and—"

"You're getting wound up all over again. Please start at the beginning. What was the gardener's name?"

"Fergus O'Malley."

Michael whistled softly. "Poor fellow," he said. "I knew him to speak to on the street, but I thought he was a gillie, not a gardener."

"He used to be," Kristy answered, recalling Liam McMurrough's remark to the Fermoy storekeeper.

"I wonder why he changed jobs?"

Kristy shrugged. "You told me yourself, Michael, that the fishing's been miserable these past few years."

"Still—" Michael started, then broke off as a strapping, auburn-haired woman come into the room, rolling up her sleeves as she said, "Sorry to keep you waiting."

"That's quite all right," Michael told her, and ordered. When she came back with a pot of hot tea and two cups, he asked conversationally, "Have you been to the funeral? I've just been hearing about Fergus O'-Malley's strange death."

Kristy knew that by now everyone in Ballyhooly could recognize her as one of the Americans staying at the castle, so she wasn't surprised when the barmaid said, "Strange is the word for it," and added, "You must have been the one who found him, miss."

"It was my brother, actually," Kristy said, "but I was right behind."

The barmaid tucked a straying lock back into her hairdo. "It must have given you a turn, him lying there. Is it likely he could have slipped and fallen, as some say, or do you think he met with foul play?"

"I haven't the slightest idea," Kristy admitted, not at all loathe to discuss the tragedy. "Your guess is as good as mine."

"Well, my guess is the man was done in by somebody he'd angered, and there was plenty of those. Fergus was never a type you took to, even when he was young. Pat O'Malley, on the other hand, is a sweet man if there ever was one."

135

"What made Fergus so unpopular?" Kristy dared to ask.

"His manner, partly. He always had a chip on his shoulder."

"But that wasn't all?" Kristy probed.

The barmaid hesitated, then said, "You might say he was sore at the world, everything and everybody. Many's the time he's stood at that bar arguing that the laws were all wrong, that they favored the rich and ground down the poor, and he for one wouldn't stand for it. Not he!"

"There's more than a mite of justification for his attitude," Michael put in. "You'll have to admit that."

"Oh, I'll admit it fast enough," said the barmaid, "but a man can't take the law into his own hands and twist it and undo it. Not unless he aims to land in jail."

"Right," Michael agreed. "But Fergus may have been one of those who did a lot of talking—all bark and no bite, you might say."

A gust of wind blew through the opened door to the pub's main room, and with it came several villagers, two women among them. The barmaid excused herself and went to greet them, while Kristy and Michael sipped their tea and listened shamelessly.

"Pour us a pint all round," ordered a man's deep voice. "After standing in the damp of that graveyard, we're needing a bit of cheer."

"You skipped out early, Cora," a woman said teasingly.

"And why not? I have my bar to tend."

"Well," said another man, "I'm glad it's all over. Sure, and Fergus had rubbed the bottom of his purse till his fingers were raw. Now he won't be standing here complaining about his lot any more."

"His lot was no worse than ours," put in the second woman. "He just made it seem so by grumbling all the time."

"It's my opinion Fergus was something of a miser," said the man with the deep voice. "He made good enough money when he was the colonel's gillie, and the gardener's job at the castle isn't a bad one. He got the house and a living wage."

"But he always wanted more than he had," said the barmaid, Cora. "Even as a lad he was greedy. I remember once—" She broke off and said, "Never mind what I remember. We shouldn't be speaking ill of the dead."

To Kristy's disappointment, this ended the conversation about the gardener. She and Michael finished their tea, paid up and left, going across the street to retrieve Michael's bicycle before they set out for the castle.

"Let me have a ride," Kristy begged. "I haven't been on a bike since we left Oregon."

She went coasting down the short hill that led to Ballyhooly's park gate, then came pumping back. "I wonder if I can rent a bike in the village?" she called to Michael. "We could take a picnic someday and go off on an excur-

137

sion." Glancing at the sky, she added, "If the sun ever comes out."

"If you wait for the sun to shine in Ireland, you'll wait your life away," said Michael. "I think you've got a grand idea, Kristy. And if you can't find a bicycle in Ballyhooly, you can certainly get one in Fermoy."

"Where could we go?"

Michael shrugged. "We could make it to Mallow and back, if you like. There's an interesting old abbey not far from Castletownroche along the way."

Kristy fell in with this suggestion at once. "When can we go? Tomorrow?" she asked.

"Any time you say, unless it's pouring rain."

"Does your aunt have a phone?" Kristy asked.

"Yes, fortunately."

"Oh, good! Then we can keep in touch."

Michael, walking his bike along the castle driveway, raised his eyes to admire the tower. "That's a beauty, isn't it?" he murmured appreciatively. "Even the crenellation is still intact."

Kristy nodded. "Inside, though, it's sort of a disappointment." She told him how the whole family had trooped up to the top, and described the neglect and damp rot encountered on each floor. Then, chancing the fact that he might laugh at her, she told him about the light Sam had discovered, shining from within the tower during the middle of the night.

138

"What night was this?" Michael asked.

"Christmas eve. The night of Fergus O'Malley's death. And the strange thing is, at the midnight service I heard a village woman predict that the ghost would be walking at the very time."

"I don't doubt it a bit." Michael's voice was faintly sarcastic. "Most of the Irish believe firmly in ghost stories, just as they believe in fairies, leprechauns, and banshees."

"Don't you?"

Michael shook his head. "Of course not. What good's an education if you stay as superstitious as the country people? You know as well as I do, Kristy, that the light was real."

"Then you believe me!"

"Of course I believe you. Why wouldn't I? It's curious, though. What could a prowler want in that tower at night?"

"I've thought and thought," said Kristy, "and I can't imagine. Oh, Michael, I've got lots more to tell you, but it will have to wait until we have more time alone."

After Michael parked his bicycle, she led him across the courtyard and into the house, which seemed warm and welcoming after the chill wind blowing outside. Someone had turned on the Christmas tree lights, and they twinkled bravely, while every ornament swung in the breeze from the opened door.

Kristy's parents, acquainted with Michael, were both

surprised and pleased to see him. He was introduced to
the rest of the family and duly invited for lunch, where
he sat between Aunt Irene and Grandma and managed
to charm them both. They had a dozen questions about
County Cork, to which he managed to supply most of the
answers. "You see," he explained, "I've been coming to
visit my Aunt Sheila since I was old enough to travel
alone. I love this part of the country, especially the Blackwater River. I used to want to be a gillie when I grew up."

"The way kids in the United States want to be fire-
men?" Sam asked.

"That's right."

"What are you interested in now, Michael?" Kristy's
father inquired.

"Ecology, sir. I'm hoping to go to Trinity College next
year."

"What's ecology?" Sam looked at Michael with genu-
ine curiosity.

"It's a science dealing with environment, Sam. If that
means anything to you."

"It doesn't," Sam muttered, and helped himself to
another piece of Irish bread, while Michael went on to
explain that he was concerned with conservation, and in
combating air and water pollution. "Here in Ireland, this
is quite a new field," he said.

"But a growing one!" interjected Grandpa approvingly,
and told Michael about the dying salmon he and Kristy

had discovered in the river. "The fish was obviously diseased," he said, "but the question is, why? And who can suggest a cure?"

"That's precisely the sort of thing in which I'm interested," Michael said, while Kristy sat regarding him in unconcealed admiration. He seemed old for his years compared with American boys, a young man almost, full of a man's concern for the country of his birth.

At that moment the telephone rang, with an old-fashioned tinkle that Kristy failed to recognize. Sam, however, pushed back his chair and was ready to leap to answer it, when his grandmother shook her head. "You stay here, dear. Mary will take it in the kitchen."

Less than a minute later Mary appeared in the dining room, where Nora was about to serve dessert. "Excuse me, Mr. Henderson," she said to Kristy's grandfather, "but could you come to the phone, sir? Sergeant Walsh is on the line."

Conversation languished while a pudding was passed. Kristy's parents exchanged a glance she couldn't interpret. Sam sat knocking his heels together impatiently. Aunt Irene concentrated on wiping Ned's sticky hands with a napkin. Uncle Robert said he knew someone who was getting very sleepy. Although she said it looked delicious, Gramdma refused the pudding, because she was watching her weight.

Finally, Grandpa came back and sat down, pulling in

141

his chair and putting his napkin back across his knees. There was an unaccustomed frown creasing his forehead as he said, "Well, you may as well know that the results of the autopsy on Fergus O'Malley are rather disturbing. It seems that the cause of death was poison, rather than a blow on the head."

10

Reaction to this announcement was instantaneous.

"Fergus O'Malley again!" complained Grandma. "Will he never leave us in peace?"

"He's the *real* ghost of Ballyhooly, if you ask me," said Uncle Robert with a wry chuckle. He pushed back his chair, walked around the table and picked up Ned, cradling the sleepy child against his shoulder. "I'll put him down for his nap, Irene. You stay here."

Aunt Irene agreed thankfully, then returned to the subject at hand. "Poison," she said thoughtfully as her husband left the room. "What kind of poison? Do they know?"

Grandpa shook his head. "It hasn't been determined, Sergeant Walsh said."

Sam's eyes grew large with excitement. "I was reading

143

a book about Indians, and it said there's a poison called curare—"

"Sh, Sam!" cautioned his father, intercepting a predictably long story. "Let's leave that until later. I think Grandpa has something else to say."

"Only this. Sergeant Walsh would like us to be available this afternoon. All of us," Grandpa said, with a sly glance at Kristy. "He has a few more questions he'd like to ask."

This was Michael's cue to leave as soon as lunch was over. "I'll ring you up tonight," he told Kristy as they left the dining room. "And I'll also inquire about renting another bike."

Nora, who was clearing the table, overheard. "You're welcome to borrow my bicycle any time you like, Miss Kristy," she offered.

"Oh, may I, Nora? That would be wonderful! Michael and I want to take a picnic lunch and ride to Mallow and back."

"That's quite a distance!" Nora warned. "Nine miles each way."

"Are there hills?" Kristy asked.

"Only a few short ones."

"Then I can manage," Kristy decided. "And do you think Mrs. Quinn would pack us a lunch, the way she did for the group going to the races?"

"I'm sure she'd be glad to, Miss Kristy, if you let her

know in the morning right after breakfast. There's always enough cold meat and cheese for a few sandwiches."

Michael added his thanks to Kristy's, said good-bye to the family, and started back to Fermoy just as Sergeant Walsh and another officer tramped across the courtyard to the castle. From inside, Kristy heard the bicycle wheels crunch on the gravel as she opened the door for the gardai. Privately, she was praying that tomorrow would be a clear day!

Then her attention was returned to the mystery of Fergus O'Malley's hapless death. In contrast to his former friendliness, Sergeant Walsh conducted himself in a no-nonsense manner. He introduced his companion as Superintendent Kelly from Cork, and matched his demeanor to that of the thin, beak-nosed man who gravely shook hands with each member of the family in turn.

Grandma was unusually brusque when she greeted the officers. "I hope you'll be as quick as possible," she said to Sergeant Walsh. "You understand that we're here on a holiday, and that this is not an especially amusing way to spend an afternoon."

"Of course, ma'am. I'll try to be brief. And to save time, may Superintendent Kelly have permission to go over the house while I do the interviewing?"

"You mean make a search?" Grandma's voice rose in indignation. "But why?"

"It's only routine, Mrs. Henderson," said Superintendent Kelly. "You needn't be concerned I'll disturb anything, I'd just like to take a look around."

Grandpa said, "Let's get this thing over with, Christine. There's no sense to objecting when they'll go ahead anyway."

Grandma rang the bell for Nora and asked her to show Superintendent Kelly around, while Sergeant Walsh got out his familiar notebook and stationed himself on the same stool he had occupied on his first visit to the castle, three days before. Today, however, he announced that he would like to interview each person separately.

"Then I think you'd better use the small anteroom off the main hall," said Grandma briskly. "The rest of us will wait in here where it's decently warm."

"Anything you say, ma'am." The segeant left with Grandpa in tow, while Kristy went over to the bay window and stood gazing down the river toward Fermoy, and Sam inveigled his father into starting a game of chess.

Aunt Irene curled up on the sofa with a paperback, Kristy's mother picked up the needlepoint she was working on at off moments, but Grandma paced restlessly back and forth in front of the fire. "I consider this both a nuisance and an indignity," she said, speaking to her daughter and daughter-in-law. "What possible connection could we have with the whole unfortunate affair?"

"We were here when it happened," her son reminded her, as he and Sam set up the chessmen.

"Well, I hope this sees an end to it!"

Kristy had rarely seen her grandmother in such a testy mood. Although Michael's abrupt leave-taking had been a disappointment, she herself was fascinated by the storybook quality of the proceedings. Policemen in the house questioning each member of the family, the gardener's death due to a strange and as yet unidentified poison, the possibility of a murder trial in which they might be key witnesses—and all of it happening in an Irish castle. What a tale she would have to tell the girls at home!

The chess players had barely made their opening gambits when Uncle Robert came into the room. His wife glanced up. "Asleep?" she asked in the verbal shorthand they frequently used when speaking of Ned.

He nodded, then asked, "Where's Nora off to with the new cop?"

"The house is being searched, dear. Apparently it's merely routine."

"It's perfectly ridiculous, that's what it is!" Kristy's grandmother stopped pacing and perched on the edge of a Heppelwhite side chair, looking as though she might decide to take flight at any moment.

Kristy turned from the window in time to catch her uncle's reaction to the news of the search. For a split second his eyes flickered with concern; then he frowned and half turned toward the door.

"Sergeant Walsh wants us all to wait in here," Aunt

Irene said. "He's interviewing us one by one today." Then she chuckled mischievously. "Apparently he thinks somebody's holding out on him. Have you a guilty secret, Robert?"

The question was rhetorical, Kristy realized, but apparently her uncle intended to reply, when Grandpa interrupted by calling from the doorway, "Your turn, Christine. And try not to give the poor fellow a hard time. He's only doing his duty."

"Hmph!" Grandma got to her feet and swept out of the room, her head high, her eyes blazing, while Grandpa shook his head and murmured, "Tch, tch, tch!" in obvious pity for Sergeant Walsh. Then he went over and put an arm across Kristy's shoulders. "I hope this won't spoil your afternoon."

Kristy knew that he was referring, indirectly, to Michael. "Oh, no. Actually, I think it's all rather exciting. I feel like a character in one of Aunt Irene's mysteries."

"Except this is not fiction, Kristy. It's real." Aunt Irene earmarked a page in her paperback and put the book on a side table. "And it's certainly no time to be frivolous."

Surprised by her aunt's tone of reproof, Kristy stammered, "I—I didn't mean—"

Her grandfather cut off her apology by squeezing her shoulder affectionately. "Of course you didn't, darling, but Irene's right. If poor Fergus was poisoned, the suspicion of murder looms even larger than before."

148

"Murder?" Sam arrested in midair a chess move he was about to make, and swung around to accost his grandfather with large eyes.

"The suggestion is bound to come up, Sammy," his father said, sitting back in his chair. "I'm sorry you're involved in this, but it can't be helped. Just remember to answer Sergeant Walsh's questions carefully and truthfully. Then maybe this afternoon will end our harrassment."

Kristy, for the first time, caught the resemblance between her father and her grandmother. At heart they were not as collected as they appeared to be on the surface; each was upset by the disturbance of the family's privacy.

Grandpa, on the other hand, tended to be more easygoing. "Now the lads at the pub will really have something to talk about!" he mused as he went over to poke up the fire.

The chess players went back to their game, while Uncle Robert dropped into a deep lounge chair and sat staring at the flames. He looked unhappy about something, curiously disturbed, Kristy thought, and wondered what—aside from the return of the police—could have upset him? Usually Uncle Robert seemed abstracted in company. He lived in a world of his own, with little to say, unless the conversation touched on a subject that truly interested him or he found an opportunity to make one

149

of his sly jokes. Kristy was struck by the fact that she had never before seen him sit idle; usually he had a book in his hand.

At this moment Grandma opened the drawing-room door, looking—to everyone's relief—slightly mollified. "Sergeant Walsh will see you next, Stephen," she said. "Apparently he's taking us in the order of seniority."

Kristy's mother glanced up from her needlepoint and watched her husband leave the room, an expression of pride and affection in her eyes. With a characteristic gesture she raised a hand and pushed a lock of hair back from her forehead, then, smiling at nothing in particular, drew a fresh skein of yarn from her workbasket and began to cut in into appropriate lengths.

Sam, his chess game interrupted, pushed back his chair and turned his attention to his grandmother. "You weren't gone very long." he said. "What did that guy want to know?"

"Nothing extra special."

"Do they think Fergus O'Malley was *murdered?*"

"They don't know, dear. They don't know."

Once more Kristy was reminded of her father. Mother and son had the same habit of repeating themselves.

Sam subsided, with a sigh, and sat kicking his heels against the chair legs until his mother said, "Stop that, Sam."

When her father came back, looking puzzled, Kristy

150

went over and sat on the sofa beside Aunt Irene, while her grandmother and grandfather exchanged a glance she couldn't interpret. Were they conspiratorial? Certainly they weren't amused.

Time dragged. Kristy's mother returned, nodded to Uncle Robert, and took up her needlepoint without comment. Aunt Irene began to twist her hands restlessly, then got up and walked the length of the room, touching an ornament here and there, adusting the angle of a stack of magazines, straightening a picture.

"This is becoming a bore," she said finally.

Grandma nodded, and glanced at her watch. "I couldn't agree more."

When her aunt's turn came, Kristy herself became slightly edgy. What would Sergeant Walsh ask? What more could she tell that she hadn't already told? There was the light she had seen in the tower, the discovery of Fergus's brown cap, and the missing pages from the book of ghost stories, but now these tidbits seemed extraneous to the real issue—that a man was dead who might have been poisoned by a person or persons unknown.

I'm beginning even to *think* in terms of detective fiction, she scolded herself as she awaited her own turn, then walked down the hall on knees unexpectedly limp.

Sergeant Walsh said, "Ah, sit down, Miss Christine." He fumbled with his notebook and peered at her over the steel frames of his spectacles, which changed his appearance and made him seem more professional than constabular. Kristy smiled and took the chair indicated, feeling suddenly at ease.

"This won't take long," said the sergeant. "First of all I must tell you that the toxicology laboratory in Cork has discovered traces in the deceased of a poison that as yet is unidentified. There is no doubt, however, that this poison was the cause of death, which leads us to believe that our investigation should continue, and, in fact, its scope be broadened."

He delivered this statement in a monotone that fascinated Kristy, even though her mind repudiated the actual words. However, she nodded and tried to look intelligent, and the sergeant seemed pleased.

"Good," he said, as though she had indicated understanding of an algebraic equation. "What I must ask you is this: can you think of anything that has happened at Ballyhooly since your arrival that might conceivably have any bearing on Fergus O'Malley's death?"

Kristy shook her head, her long hair swinging against her shoulders, her eyes solemn. "Not really," she murmured.

Sergeant Walsh sighed, as though this were to be expected. "Can you think of anything—anything at all—untoward?"

"Unto what?"

"Untoward. Unusual shall we say?"

152

"Well, maybe this isn't important at all, but then again, maybe it is. While I was walking with my grandfather on the other side of the river on Christmas day I found a brown cloth cap, the kind that Fergus used to wear, down by the bank."

"Where is it now?"

"I gave it to Mrs. O'Malley. She says it did belong to Fergus, actually, so that means he must have been across the river sometime in the past few days."

"Thank you," murmured Sergeant Walsh with a trace of a smile. "Is there anything else that you've discovered?"

Kristy hesitated, then blurted, "There is the business of the ghost."

"What about the ghost?" asked the constable, appearing unsurprised.

"Well," said Kristy, feeling a trifle foolish, "the story, 'Ballyhooly's Ghostly Catch,' was torn out of the book in the castle library, and it turned up in Mr. O'Malley's bedroom, if that means anything. Maybe you ought to know, too, that Sam and I saw a light in the tower, early on Christmas morning, and who would have the key but Mr. O'Malley, who by then was dead?"

Sergeant Walsh couldn't answer this question. He seemed only mildly interested, and asked, "What time did you see a light, and exactly where?"

"Around three o'clock," Kristy said, "On the second

153

floor, then the first. It could have been a flashlight. Sam saw it first, and called me, so I'm not making this up," she added as she saw a mistrustful expression cross the constable's face.

"Your younger brother always seems to see things first," he commented. "He must be a very inquisitive child."

"Not really," said Kristy. "I'm the one who's curious. Sam just stumbles onto things."

The sergeant nodded. "Like a dead body," he said wryly. "I think that will be all, at the moment, Miss Christine."

As Kristy walked back to the drawing room she felt rather let down. Sergeant Walsh had seemed to find the information she had produced trivial, and she was rather glad she had kept a few additional items to herself. He would have made little or nothing of a donkey driver who signaled to a friend across the river. As for the dying salmon she and her grandfather had discovered, what possible connection could this have to a violent crime? Yet the sequence of incidents kept nagging her, and in spite of herself she felt that somewhere there lurked another important clue.

"Sam!" Kristy jerked a thumb toward the door she left ajar as she entered the drawing room. "You're the last."

"Although the last, not least," teased his father, as Sam took time to make a move, then said, "Check."

"King Lear, Act 1, Scene 1," murmured Grandpa, looking foxy.

"Hurry up, Sam," urged his grandmother. "We're all getting tired of sitting around. Don't let the sergeant involve you in a long-winded discussion. It's past time for my nap."

"It's not the sergeant who's apt to be long-winded," commented Kristy's father, "but I must say, that son of mine can play chess!" He sat back, ran his fingers through his hair, and stared at the board. "He's got me licked, and today I really tried."

Five minutes passed before Sam reappeared, followed by Sergeant Walsh and Superintendent Kelly, who was carrying a small, rather battered can in his left hand.

"Does anyone here recognize this?" he asked as he entered the room and put the can down on the nearest table.

Along with the rest of the family, Kristy stared at the tin, which once might have contained baking powder, judging from its size and shape. The paper wrapper must have been ripped off long ago, because the can was dented and rusted. Superintendent Kelly turned it slowly in a half circle, then tilted it to reveal the top. With a red marking pencil someone had scrawled the word POISON and followed it with an exclamation point.

Kristy stifled a gasp, and looked up to find Superintendent Kelly's glance sweeping the room. For several seconds nobody spoke. Then Grandma said hopefully, "It could be rat poison, I suppose. Where did you find it—in the scullery?"

The officer shook his head, looking increasingly solemn. "I rather doubt it, Mrs. Henderson. A container of rat poison would be clearly marked." He paused for a moment longer, then turned to Kristy's father. "You're quite sure you don't recognize this tin?" he asked insistently.

Stephen Henderson shrugged and shook his head. "Never saw it before in my life, Superintendent."

"Yet it was found on the shelf of your bedroom wardrobe, tucked back in the corner, hidden—you might say —from the light of day."

Every eye turned toward Kristy's father, who reflected for a moment or two before replying. "Really?" he asked easily. "I hadn't noticed, but then I'm rather vague about housekeeping details, as my wife can corroborate. I suppose we can assume the can was there when we arrived."

"I'm afraid we can assume nothing of the sort, Mr. Henderson. Nora says she cleaned each bedroom thoroughly, and that nothing at all was left in the wardrobes. Both Mrs. Quinn and the second maid, Mary, can vouch for the fact that she's a very thorough housekeeper."

"No doubt, no doubt." To Kristy's relief, her father's tone sounded completely normal.

"Very well, then we agree that somebody placed the tin

at the rear of the wardrobe shelf," growled the Superintendent ominously.

Stephen Henderson nodded, still unperturbed.

"And the most logical person to have hidden it there was you." The officer's forefinger jabbed the air in the direction of the professor's chest.

"Logical? It depends on your definition of logic, Superintendent. If you consider that logical means reasonable and indeed possible, I'll have to agree, but if you define the word as meaning plausible or credible in the Aristotelian sense, I must disagree most emphatically."

As Stephen Henderson spoke, Superintendent Kelly lowered his finger jerkily, an inch or so at a time. Finally his hand hung limply at this side while his face was a study in conflicting emotions. He looked annoyed but stubborn, confused but intent, and Kristy began to feel sorry for him, because the policeman had no weapon to combat her father's argument.

"You claim, Mr. Henderson, that you didn't put the tin on the closet shelf?" the Superintendent muttered, while Sergeant Walsh made notes in his omnipresent black book.

"I do."

"Then who did? It was one of you. It's got to be!"

Kristy glanced around the room in consternation. Superintendent Kelly sounded very sure of himself.

From a corner chair, to the cushioned depths of which

Uncle Robert had retreated with the book he was reading in snatches, came an unexpected reply. "I'm afraid I'm the guilty party, Superintendent."

The entire family turned toward Robert Russell in astonishment. "You?" murmured Aunt Irene.

"Then why didn't you speak up?" the officer barked.

"I have no excuse, except that it seemed possible, for a few moments, that your investigation might take an interesting turn. Besides, I was interested in the manner in which my brother-in-law fended you off. Frankly, I became absorbed in the dialogue. I apologize for having amused myself briefly at your expense, adding a little spice to an otherwise tedious afternoon."

This speech was the longest Kristy had ever heard her uncle make. Having become accustomed, by now, to his unpredictable sense of humor, she found his remarks in character. She realized, however, that Superintendent Kelly believed he was being baited and had a perfect right to be resentful. It didn't surprise her when he said, "Cut the malarkey, Mr. Russell, and give us the facts."

11

Uncle Robert's explanation, although tardy, was to the point. He claimed that twice—on the morning of Fergus O'Malley's death and again on Christmas morning—he had found the door to the salmon smokehouse at the rear of the kitchen open. Knowing that the young O'Malleys and Ned, impelled by Sam, might take it into their heads to use the small tower as a playhouse or hideaway, he went in and took a look around.

"There was a flashlight lying on a shelf just inside the door," he said, "but not much else except for the remains of a fire in the pit under the chimney. I picked up the flash and looked around. The beam shone on a glint of metal among the ashes. That's how I happened on the can. When I saw it was marked POISON I naturally decided to get it out of harm's way."

"That sounds likely enough up to a point, but why did you pin suspicion on your brother-in-law?" asked Superintendent Kelly gruffly.

Kristy saw a look of astonishment, quickly replaced by one of contained amusement, cross her uncle's face. "Have you any children, Superintendent?" he asked gently.

"What's that got to do with it?"

"I'm afraid it's a question of logic again." Uncle Robert's voice was mild and patient, as though he were trying to make up for his previous teasing manner. "Ned, our three-year-old, is a great climber—a little monkey, really—and I wanted to put the can of poison in a place he couldn't possibly reach. Neither the kitchens nor our own bedroom seemed childproof, so I tucked the tin away at the top of Mr. Henderson's closet, concluding that there it would be quite safe from prying hands." He turned to his brother-in-law. "I meant to tell you Steve, but I forgot."

Kristy's father quoted recklessly:

Of science and logic he chatters,
As fine and as fast as he can;
Though I am no judge of such matters,
I'm sure he's a talented man.

Grandpa chuckled appreciatively, but Superintendent Kelly continued to look severe. "This is no laughing matter, gentlemen," he said, and Stephen Henderson apologized at once. "I know, Superintendent. I'm sorry. But we're all getting a little keyed up, and as my mother has explained to you, this is *not* our idea of a vacation."

Superintendent Kelly bowed, then picked up the incriminating can. "We will have this powder identified at the laboratory," he said significantly. "I will be in touch with you."

Stalking out of the room, followed by Sergeant Walsh, who shot commiserating smiles at the family in a farewell volley of sympathy, the superintendent accepted his cap and coat from Nora and disappeared.

Kristy unclenched her hands and sank back on the sofa against her aunt's arm. Visibly relieved, Sam asked, "What was that all about?" Stephen Henderson and Robert Russell stood up, slapped one another on the back and grinned. "We finally routed him," Kristy's father crowed.

"You acted abominably," his sister said, glancing from one to the other, and added, for good measure, "Both of you."

Grandpa sighed. "Let the boys have their fun," he advised. "You have to admit those officers were rather tiresome."

"I'm going to take a nap," said Grandma, rising. "I'm

weary of the whole performance. And I advise any of you who can't keep your eyes open to do the same."

Following this remark, which Kristy considered ambiguous, the senior Mrs. Henderson trotted out of the room, and the rest of the group dispersed in her wake, bent on various personal and private objectives.

A drizzle had started to spatter the windowpanes, so Kristy elected to wash her hair and hope for a clear day tomorrow. She unearthed her shampoo and hurried to the bathroom, puzzled by the unexpected turn the investigation of Fergus O'Malley's death had taken.

The water was hot, the bathroom was cold, and Kristy's bedroom was positively frigid, so she went back to the drawing room and crouched by the fire with her damp hair swept forward over her face.

"Getting all spruced up for Michael?" Sam asked as he ambled in, munching a cookie.

"What's it to you?"

Sam twitched his shoulders, unwilling to admit he was jealous. "I'm glad I'm not a girl."

Kristy smiled to herself. She was distinctly glad she *was* a girl, and her satisfaction with her lot continued when she awakened the next morning to find the sun peeking from behind a cloud bank, as though trying to decide whether it was safe to come out. Michael phoned just as she finished breakfast, and arranged to be in Ballyhooly by ten o'clock, when they could start at once for Mallow.

162

Sam, who had been listening to his sister's end of the conversation, looked sour and neglected, but Kristy didn't care. "Get Rosaleen to come up and play," she suggested unctuously, to pay him back for his remark about Michael yesterday afternoon.

"Oh, go fish!" Sam went off, looking sulky, and later Kristy saw him cross the road to watch the gypsy tinker at work. She waved to him cheerfully as she and Michael wheeled out of the park gate, but his response was far from polite. The fortune-teller, however, who was climbing down a short ladder propped against the wagon's open back, turned and called a good morning, followed by the typical Irish "God bless!"

The road to Mallow was a narrow one, by American standards. Although it was surfaced, there was barely room for two cars to pass. Fortunately traffic was light, and for a mile or more at a time Kristy and Michael could ride abreast, while on either side sheep, grazing peacefully in the meadows, seemed to relish the taste of the frosty grass.

Michael was full of bounce and enthusiasm this morning. His cheeks were as red as checkerberries and his blue eyes were bright with enjoyment. "What could be more perfect?" he asked Kristy, gesticulating broadly with both hands. "The sun is shining and I'm going to spend a whole day with you."

163

Kristy was pleased but she didn't intend to show it. "Look out!" she cautioned. "You'll run off the road. No hands is for kids."

At a cluster of small whitewashed houses a truck was pulled up beside a mound of sugar beets higher than a man's head. The whitish roots, bigger than turnips, with earth still clinging to their surfaces, were being scooped into the body of the truck by a couple of boys wearing pullovers and knitted caps. Michael hailed the pair and called a good morning as he wheeled past. "How's the factory doing?" he asked as an afterthought.

"Busy as ever," one of the lads called back.

"That's a mixed blessing," Michael said to Kristy when they were out of earshot. "The sugar beet factory has given employment to quite a few young men along this reach of the Blackwater, and that's good. But the waste dumped into the river is a terrible thing. Some people think the salmon are in danger of extinction because of the pollution, although the old-timers claim poachers are primarily to blame."

Kristy nodded. "My grandfather and my uncle were talking about the same thing the night of Saint Stephen's Day," she said. "I guess when you live here you feel very strongly about the salmon, don't you?" She peered at Michael intently, because in one of his characteristic changes of mood he had suddenly become grave.

Nodding, Michael said, "And no wonder. The salmon

is a fascinating fish. I'm going to do a term paper on salmon after I get back home. Are you interested?"

"Yes, indeed," Kristy replied, more from politeness than honesty. She had been anxious to tell Michael about the can marked POISON turned up by the police, but since the whole, uncluttered day stretched ahead she supposed that could wait.

"You've never seen a salmon rise, have you, Kristy?"

"No."

"It's a magnificent sight! When the salmon obey the spawning urge they come back from the sea to the rivers where they were hatched. Only to those rivers, no others. It's as though they had memories. They swim straight upstream, and there are mighty few barricades that can stop them. I've seen a salmon rise from the depths of the river below Fermoy and hurtle over the dam like a living Polaris missile." Coasting down a slight grade toward a distant bridge, Michael grew dreamy with recollection. "It's really something to see."

Whenever Michael's enthusiasm flared, his brogue thickened. Only an Irishman, Kristy was sure, could make a description of a jumping fish sound like poetry.

At the bridge a lorry came rumbling toward them, forcing the bicyclists off the macadam. Pulling up by the mossy stone wall that served as a guardrail, Kristy peered down at the sluggish stream. "Is this still the Blackwater?" she asked.

165

"I don't think so," Michael replied, sounding a trifle uncertain. "We're in Castletowneroche, so this should be the Awbeg. It flows into the Blackwater a little farther along." He was about to remount when he paused with one foot on a pedal. "Look, Kristy. That's what I mean about pollution. See the smoke pluming up above those trees? That's the sugar beet factory. Now look at the water, not in midstream but toward the bank."

A blanket of gray froth as broad as a big rug was floating slowly downstream, the edges catching on fallen branches here and there and sluffing off the main mass. A crane perched on an overhanging tree limb stared down at the unappetizing crust. Kristy wrinkled her nose in aversion, then glanced at Michael and burst out laughing. "You and that bird have exactly the same expression on your faces," she said.

"Right. Disgust."

Because she too was repelled, Kristy felt a need to change the subject. "Oh, come on, Michael, let's stop being so serious," she complained as she got back on her bike. "Let's talk about something cheerful for a change."

The hands of the town clock, placed conveniently on the half-timbered facade of a handsome eighteenth century building, stood at high noon when the pair rode down the main street of Mallow, a town on the railroad line between Dublin and Cork. To Kristy it was more attractive than Fermoy, with a certain color and charac-

166

ter. The shops were better stocked, and the people on the streets looked substantial. Tactfully, she didn't mention this to Michael, because she suspected he had affectionate ties to his aunt's hometown.

"Is there anywhere special you'd like to go?" Michael asked Kristy.

"Yes. Dad wants me to try to find a tackle shop and ask what kind of lures are best for salmon. He has something called a royal coachman, but he isn't at all sure it's the thing."

"That's easy," said Michael. "The best one's right here on the main street. Gillies from miles around swear by it. I'll bet even Fergus O'Malley used to come here when he was alive."

A few minutes later he braked in front of a strip of sidewalk faced by a one-story building that had survived the development of the town, and led Kristy into a store so outstandingly masculine that she felt ill at ease. A thin, weatherbeaten man stood behind a counter, peering over half spectacles at a Cork newspaper, which apparently had just been delivered. Although the news appeared to fascinate him, he was willing to tear himself away for the sake of potential customers.

"Good day to ye," he said, glancing from Michael to Kristy almost suspiciously.

"You're Mr. Dermott Canty, aren't you?" asked Michael easily, stepping forward and holding out his hand.

167

"I'm Michael Curtis of Dublin, and this is Christine Henderson, whose family is staying at Ballyhooly over the holidays."

Kristy was glad that Michael hadn't said "Ballyhooly Castle." She was American enough to want to feel democratic rather than to be identified with an address that sounded pretentious.

The proprietor of the tackle shop nodded. "Pleased to make your acquaintance, miss."

"My father wanted me to find out what lures you consider best for salmon. He's anxious to go fishing as soon as the season opens."

"Well, now," said Mr. Canty, obviously pleased at being consulted. "My advice would be one thing if he was to fish at midmorning, and another if he was to fish at sunup."

The remark confounded Kristy. "What," she ventured, "would you consider the best time?"

"Sunup, by all means," said the storekeeper. "Tell him to get to the river on a misty morning at the same time the birds begin to sing. Wait until the mist begins rising off the water. Tell him to fish then for about ten minutes as if every cast is the most important one he's ever made."

Mr. Canty opened a drawer in the base of the glass counter behind which he was standing and took out a lure that he handled as though it were very precious. "I'd suggest this yellow belly for the kind of fishing I'm speak-

168

ing of," he said. "You take it back to your father and tell him Dermott Canty recommends it. And you might mention that I know what I'm talking about because I used to be a gillie myself."

Kristy hadn't intended to buy anything, only to make inquiries, but Mr. Canty's sales talk was so positive that she had no recourse. Happily, she had brought some money along in the pocket of her bluejeans, and she counted out the purchase price carefully, while Mr. Canty stood by looking unexpectedly sorry that the transaction had been so brief.

"I hear Fergus O'Malley got his a few days ago," the storekeeper said as he wrapped the lure in a twist of brown paper. "Were you at Ballyhooly when it happened, miss?"

"Yes," replied Kristy. "It was my brother who found him."

"Was it now?"

"Did you know him personally, Mr. Canty?" Michael asked.

"Fergus? Known him since he was a whippersnapper. Too bad. Good man gone sour."

"What do you mean by that?" Kristy asked, trying to keep her tone casual.

"He was a grand gillie in his day," replied the proprietor. "Not without faults, of course, but smart as they come. Then he got in with a gang of soreheads like Liam McMurrough—a bad lot if ever I saw one—and he began

169

to blame the spoiling of the river on the landowners, when it was the stroke-haulers ruining the fishing all the time."

"The what?" Kristy asked curiously.

"The stroke-haulers, miss. Poachers who fish with three-pronged barbs and rake the fish in by the score."

"Are you sure there are still stroke-haulers on the Blackwater?" asked Michael. "Or is it the sugar-beet waste that's killing the fish?"

"A bit of both, I suspect," replied Mr. Canty. "Though I shouldn't speak ill of the dead, I'd hazard a guess that Fergus O'Malley could have answered that question better than I."

"Really?" Kristy's eyes widened in surprise. Then she remembered the fishing jacket and hip boots Fergus had been wearing when he died.

Mr. Canty nodded solemnly. "Once a gillie, always a gillie, to my way of thinking. Fergus took a job as gardener at the castle when the fishing in the Blackwater fell off, but he was a man of the river, first, last and always."

"But if he loved the river, why should he want to catch fish illegally?" Kristy asked, confused.

"After he got to be a gardener," Mr. Canty said, knowingly, "Fergus began to play the horses, and it takes a powerful lot of money to feed that habit." He waggled a forefinger in caution, and glanced at each of his young customers in turn. "Besides, Fergus resented the gentry, especially the British, as he has stood right in this store

170

and told me, many's the time. He not only believed the rivers should belong to the common people, he went further. He made up his mind to spoil the fun of the rich people who own and rent out the fishing rights."

"Are you still guessing, Mr. Canty, or do you know this for a fact?" asked Michael, with a hard edge to his voice that made Kristy turn and glance at him.

Some of the fire went out of Mr. Canty's manner. "Well, I can't say I've been an actual eyewitness," he countered. "Since my arthritis started I don't go out much on the river. More times I do but most times I don't, if you understand."

Michael appeared to understand but Kristy was baffled by the colloquialism. It seemed to be a contradiction in terms. She wished that somehow she could find out whether Mr. Canty's suspicions were justifiable, because if Fergus O'Malley should prove to have been a habitual poacher, some people might well have wished him out of the way.

Meanwhile, Michael had launched on another tack. "There's a tale going around Fermoy that small-scale operations like stroke-hauling couldn't account for the loss of so many fish," he said with a return to his former easy, conversational manner. "Do you suppose that McMurrough and some of his crowd are on to something new?"

"Could be," said Mr. Canty, "and then again the rumor about poison could be just that and no more." He wasn't going to walk into a baited trap and have his word questioned twice.

Kristy came alive again. "Poison? What kind of poison?"

"Spurge, more than likely."

"What's spurge?" Kristy asked.

Before Mr. Canty could answer, another customer came banging through the door, a bluff, hearty man wearing a tweed jacket with leather patches on the elbows and a pair of riding breeches. He was obviously in a hurry, because he glanced at his watch as he crossed the floor, then addressed the proprietor apologetically. "Excuse me, Canty, but could I interrupt a moment. All I want to do is pick up that order I left with you yesterday."

"Quite all right, Mr. Tompkins, sir." Mr. Canty said, "Excuse me" to Kristy and Michael and turned to his valued older customer.

"What's spurge?" Kristy asked again in a whisper to Michael. "Could that be the poison in the can?"

"What can?" asked Michael in his turn. Then they both burst out laughing.

"I'll clue you in," Kristy promised, "as soon as we're outside."

Meanwhile, the brief transaction had been completed and the customer had hurried off. "Do you know who that was?" Mr. Canty asked Michael. "Mr. Grantley G.

172

Tompkins, owner of the big sugar beet factory down the road."

Michael was unimpressed. "So *he's* the guy who's dumping all the garbage in the river!" he exclaimed.

"He claims it's the poachers that have ruined the fishing, not the factory residue," replied Mr. Canty. "As a matter of fact, Mr. Tompkins said in my presence, just the other day, that if the *gardai* could stop the poaching he'd make arrangements to bury his waste."

"Well, that's a challenge!" said Michael, mollified.

As soon as they had said good-bye and emerged on the street, Kristy quickly brought her companion up-to-date on the developments of the previous afternoon, then asked again, "Could the poison in the can be spurge?"

To her disappointment, Michael shook his head. "A can that size wouldn't hold enough spurge to knock out a minnow."

"O.K. I'll go back to my first question. What *is* spurge?" Kristy asked as they pedaled back along the road to Ballyhooly in search of a picnic spot.

"It's a plant—actually a weed around here—something like Saint-John's-wort."

"Very informational, since I'm not acquainted with Saint John's wart or warts or even Saint John."

Michael grinned. "W-o-r-t, stupid."

"Oh."

"Anyway, there's a rumor that spurge roots and stems

173

can be chopped up, packed in gunnysacks, then trampled by foot in shallow water. A milky substance leaks out, and this stuff affects a salmon like a dose of knock-out drops. They say a fellow with a couple of sacks of spurge can poison a mile of the river. Then what could be easier than to scoop the anesthetized salmon up with nets?"

Kristy shuddered. "It's so unfair!"

"On two counts," Michael agreed. "It's unfair to the fishermen who have paid to fish these particular waters, and it's also unfair to the fish, who aren't given even a sporting chance."

Kristy rode on for a few minutes in silence. "Michael?" she said at last.

"Yes?"

"I'll bet Fergus O'Malley *was* mixed up with the poaching racket, and I even think there's a way we could prove it. Will you help?"

12

Kristy was quite aware that her appeal for help would have touched a far less tender heart than Michael's. With eyes as soft and green as the meadows along the Blackwater, she managed to reinforce his interest in ecology with his desire to please her as a girl.

It was lovely to be admired—lovely and somewhat heady—because mixed with the investigation they agreed to share came a newly acquired sense of feminine power. She let Michael sweep the debris from a damp and rotting log conveniently located on the riverbank before she sat down. She spread a paper bag out on the ground and set the sandwiches on it, then patted the log by her side and invited him to join her, not at all displeased when he came and sat quite close.

Yet this was no time for romance. Kristy wanted to

review the developments. "Since yesterday," she said, "we've known for sure that Fergus was poisoned. If the stuff in the can is the same as the poison found in the autopsy, Uncle Robert is bound to be suspected of murder, even if he's innocent as a newborn lamb."

"But the *gardai* must realize there's no motive."

Kristy cocked her head to one side, thoughtful, then dubious. "Isn't there something called circumstantial evidence that weighs heavily in a case like this?"

"There is indeed," said Michael with a grin. "Maybe you should go into law."

Kristy ignored the jibe and started off on a series of conjectures. "Who could have wanted Fergus out of the way? Another poacher? It doesn't seem likely." She stared across the gorse-strewn pasture toward the dark water. "A gillie who is being done out of a job because the fishing is poor? I doubt that, too. A man doesn't commit murder unless he's personally involved."

"Not likely," agreed Michael. "Nor are any of the big landowners apt to get worked up to the point of popping off a poacher. The goodies making away with the baddies —wouldn't that be a switch?"

"Besides, Fergus wasn't popped. He was poisoned."

"So he was." Michael selected another sandwich from Mrs. Quinn's generous supply.

"What would a load of spurge look like?" Kristy asked as he took his first bite.

"Something like a load of laurel or any other kind of brush," said Michael when he could speak. "Not very interesting."

"Could it be carried by a donkey?"

"Of course. Or by a man, for that matter. Even a big load would be pretty light."

Kristy described the incident she had watched from the castle tower, trying to remember whether the driver of the panniered donkey had been tall or short, fat or thin. She told Michael about the signal exchanged with someone—Fergus perhaps?—on the Ballyhooly side of the river, and wondered whether the bags could conceivably have contained spurge.

"Anything's possible," Michael said, "but it seems to me you're indulging in wishful thinking. We've got to deal with facts, not conjecture, Kristy. Don't tell me you hoped to prove O'Malley was a poacher through this one episode?"

Kristy bit her lip, anxious that she not lose stature in Michael's eyes. "But if we could find the bags," she persisted, "and if they really did contain spurge?"

"That would be different," Michael agreed, "but we'd still have to establish the probability that the sacks were in the gardener's possession. Not too easy."

"Nothing is easy," Kristy sighed, "although there is the evidence of the cap." Besides, she took heart from the fact that Michael had used the word "we" rather than

177

"you." He was committed to being an ally, and this lent zest to the business of playing detective. "Let's think where those sacks could be," she said. "The tower, the boathouse, the rock garden—"

"The graveyard?"

"Why might they be there?" Kristy asked, puzzled.

Michael shrugged. "Fergus was found there, wasn't he?"

"At least we could look," Kristy agreed, although the prospect of revisiting the crooked rows of somber stones did not appeal to her. "Maybe when we get back . . . ?"

Glancing at the sky, Michael reminded her that it was time to be on their way, and suggested that they visit the abbey on another day. He set a stiff pace on the road home. Even so, by the time they reached Ballyhooly the sun was sinking low in the western sky. "I've got to be pushing along," he said at the castle gate, "if I want to make it to Fermoy before dark." Calling over his shoulder, "I'll ring you up tomorrow," he hurried off.

Wearily, Kristy wheeled her bike across the cattle guard and up the drive. The calves of her legs ached, and there was a chill in the air that made her shiver. From across the road came the pungent smell of burning wood from the gypsies' campfire, and from the foot of the garden the stones of the graveyard gleamed in the dying light. She had no desire to prowl among them alone this evening. Besides, she was too tired.

Inside the castle, everyone was again drinking tea in the drawing room. Kristy accepted a cup gratefully, delivered the purchase she had made for her father, and answered questions about the trip to Mallow, omitting any mention of the new evidence she hoped to uncover concerning Fergus O'Malley's questionable past.

The family was making plans to go off on an excursion to the Rock of Cashel on the following morning. Here, Saint Patrick's Cathedral, started in the eleventh century and now a picturesque ruin, was a sight everyone wanted to see.

Maps were consulted, distances estimated, and a picnic lunch considered. It was assumed that Kristy would go along, but when she awakened with a slight head cold the next morning, she begged off, offering to take care of Ned while secretly she awaited Michael's telephone call. She planned to invite him to lunch at the castle, after which, with Ned tucked in for his nap, they would have a couple of hours to search the grounds for two sacks which might or might not contain spurge, and any other clues the *gardai* might possibly have missed.

Michael was late in phoning. "I overslept," he excused himself. "After all, I rode twelve kilometers farther than you did yesterday."

Kristy's heart fell. "Does that mean you can't come over?"

"Not at all. I'm just waiting for you to invite me,

although I'd like to give Aunt Sheila a hand with some outdoor chores before I start off."

Yesterday's sun, in setting, had made an idle promise to shine again today. The two cars started for Cashel in a fine drizzle, which seemed to discourage no one. Nora, who had tucked the picnic hampers into the trunks at the last minute, even seemed to find the weather favorable, commenting equably, "It's a grand soft day, thank God."

Ned screamed briefly in dismay at his mother's desertion, but to Kristy's relief he didn't cry real tears, and was smiling again by the time the tires stopped crunching on the drive. She said, "Come on, let's take a walk," and he held her hand happily while she led him along the path to the graveyard and in through the creaking gate.

The ground was trampled around the spot where the gardener's body had lain, but otherwise the place looked undisturbed. Ned, too young to associate fear or distaste with the leaning gravestones, scampered among them, playing hide-and-seek with his cousin and shouting with delight when she gave chase.

Remarkably nimble for a three-year-old, he led her up a grassy slope toward a stand of rhododendrons bordering the stone wall that closed off the castle park from the road. Ducking in and out among the leafy branches, he came up short against the wrought-iron gate, and here Kristy caught him. "You're a monkey!" she cried as she clasped his squirming body firmly with both hands.

He broke loose and tumbled on the ground. "Stand up, Ned. You'll catch cold," Kristy warned, conscious of her own scratchy throat. Then she glanced down at the spot where they were both standing. The rough grass was flattened in a swath about four feet wide, as though a large bundle had been dragged up the slope. The tips of every dead weed and every grass blade faced toward the grave-yard gate.

Kristy's heart leaped in excitement. She must show this to Michael. It might mean nothing at all, but again it might be important. Who could tell?

Was it possible that the bags of spurge carried by the donkey had been brought here, then disposed of, either before or after Fergus O'Malley's death?

The state of the grass supported the latter hypothesis. If something had been dragged over this ground several days ago the intermittent rains would have coaxed the vegetation upright again.

"Let's play!" Ned shouted, but Kristy scarcely heard him. She was still staring downward, hypnotized.

"Play!" Ned repeated, to no avail. Kristy was no longer in a mood for monkeyshines. "We were going for a walk, remember?" she asked him, abstractedly, and went over to try the gate.

It didn't surprise her, especially, to find it unlatched. With Ned's mittened hand safely in her grasp, Kristy went through, skidded down the slippery, moss-encrusted

181

steps to the road, and turned up toward the gypsy encampment, just visible on the other side.

Only one villager was standing by this morning, waiting for a bucket to be mended. Repair jobs for the tinker had apparently fallen off. His wife was carrying a nose bag of grain toward the tethered horse. The baby, bundled in an assortment of strange garments that presumably kept him warm, was toddling heavily after her.

Ned's quick eyes took in the tinker, the woman, and the painted wagon, then came to rest on the gypsy child, the first creature he had seen for some time who was younger than he. Tugging at Kristy's hand, he urged her forward. "Look!" he cried. "Baby! Come see!"

Kristy allowed herself to be dragged along until she realized that, although Ned was entranced, the gypsy baby was terrified. Too swaddled in clothing to make haste toward his mother, he suddenly sank to the wet ground and bawled at the top of his lungs.

The gypsy woman turned, put down the nose bag, and came back to pick him up. "Sh!" she chided, comforting him by stroking his back gently. "They won't hurt you. See the pretty American missy? And look at the little boy. He only wants to play."

"Play!" Ned shouted vociferously, eliciting fresh screams from the frightened child.

"I'm sorry," Kristy apologized. "Ned, we've scared the little boy. Come along with me now. Look! Is that Michael coming down the hill on a bicycle? Don't you want to see Michael? We've got to get along home."

The bicyclist wasn't Michael, but Ned's attention was diverted. Although he hung back, glancing over his shoulder from time to time at the captivating, black-haired bundle of rags, he allowed his cousin to lead him across the macadam and up the castle drive as far as the gardener's house. There he spotted Breeda, peeking from behind a starched curtain, and began to call her name. A moment later Mrs. O'Malley appeared at the door and invited him in, to Kristy's considerable relief.

Although Michael was late in arriving, he was brimming with news. "I've just had a talk about Liam McMurrough," he told Kristy at once, "and I may have learned a thing or two."

"Like what?"

"Well, for one thing, he knew Fergus O'Malley a good deal better than he's been giving out."

Kristy's eyebrows raised a fraction of an inch and her mind leaped back to her one encounter with Liam, on the day before Christmas, when he had called Fergus a mean man and a bitter one, while at the same time disclaiming any close acquaintanceship.

"Aunt Sheila hears most of the gossip in Fermoy," Michael continued, "and she told me there was a time last fall when the castle was empty and Liam was out of work.

Who do you think he turned to? Fergus. And Fergus took him in and let him sleep in the tower. So why should McMurrough revile him after he's dead?"

Kristy hadn't the slightest idea and said so.

"They had a falling out, that's why, a fight in a pub that all of Fermoy must have heard of, because it happened there, not in Ballyhooly, on a wet November night when there wasn't a star in the sky. Apparently Seamus O'-Rourke, another of McMurrough's buddies, was the cause of it all, but nobody seems to know what started the argument. Anyway, it ended with a good deal of glass flying, and Liam McMurrough wound up in the hospital with a badly slashed face."

"Was it Fergus O'Malley's fault?"

"McMurrough contends it was, although there was a regular free-for-all. The *gardai* couldn't decide who was responsible, so they let the whole bunch off."

"It's strange that nobody mentioned this," Kristy mused. "Neither Nora, nor Mary, nor Mrs. O'Malley—"

"Mrs. O'Malley would be the last person to mention it," Michael broke in. "After all, Fergus was her brother-in-law, and even though she may not have thought much of him, the Irish protect their own. As for the maids, they don't talk about such things to foreigners. Why should they think you'd be interested?"

"How long did Liam live in the tower?" Kristy asked.

"All of November, Aunt Sheila thinks. He moved out right after the fight."

"I wish we could find out what that fight was about," Kristy said with a sigh.

"So do I," Michael muttered.

"It *could* have been Liam McMurrough in the tower that night, don't you agree? He could have been looking for something he'd left."

"Or something he knew Fergus had hidden there."

"What could that be?"

Michael shook his head. "Search me. We seem to have reached another dead end."

At that moment Ned was brought home by Rosaleen because it was lunch time, and Nora appeared in the doorway to suggest that she feed him in the nursery so that Kristy and Michael could, as she put it, "eat in a little peace."

"I've put him down for his nap, too," she told Kristy as she served lunch in the dining room later. "I didn't undress him, just threw a comforter over him. He seemed to be dead on his feet."

Lingering at the table over fruit and coffee, Kristy and Michael talked more about school affairs than about the mystery surrounding Fergus. Finally, however, Kristy returned to the subject. Pushing back her chair, she said, "Let's take a quick look around while Ned is still asleep. There's something I want to show you."

She led Michael down to the graveyard, and up the far slope, where she pointed out the flattened grass, and proposed the theory that bags of spurge might have been dragged across here to the gate.

"It's a neat idea," Michael agreed, although his blue eyes failed to kindle with enthusiasm. "The trouble is, Kristy, it's only an idea. We haven't a shred of evidence to go on."

Defensively, Kristy said, "If we don't have evidence, ideas are better than nothing."

Michael laughed. "Don't pout. Would it take long to show me the boathouse?"

Kristy shook her head. "Ned usually sleeps for at least an hour and a half." She started down the slope, then glanced back toward the gate and said, "Oh, look, there go the gypsies. They've been camped across the road for several days now. I'm going to miss them."

The painted wagon, headed downhill toward the bridge, flashed past the grille and was gone as quickly as it had appeared. Kristy led Michael back along the lower path, skirting the rock garden and winding down to the boathouse, half hidden among tangled vines and trees. Above and to the right, from among a stand of beech, rose the chapel spire, and from the boathouse itself, to Kristy's astonishment, came the sound of laughter.

Two teen-aged boys were squatting just inside the open door, cleaning fishing rods. They rose when Kristy appeared and greeted her politely. Then, because she looked so surprised to see them, the elder explained, "We're rod boys, miss. We always come down here a few days before the season opens, just to check things out."

"Have you found anything amiss?" Michael asked.

"Nothing to speak of. Although the padlock on the rear door seems to be broken. You might mention it to Nora, if you will. Mr. O'Malley used to see to things like that, but now that he's gone—"

"I'll be glad to tell Nora about it," Kristy promised, while Michael prowled around with his hands in his pockets, walking among the neatly ranged boats and examining the fishing rods and nets hung on the wall.

He came back, after a while, and in fishermen's jargon Kristy found incomprehensible, stood in the doorway discussing gaffs and tailers with the boys. When she yawned openly he took the hint and said, "I guess we'd better be going," then added in an undertone as they climbed back uphill to the castle, "There's no doubt that one of those boats was in the water recently, but there's nothing else suspicious that I could see."

"Except the broken padlock," Kristy reminded him.

"Well, there is that, yes. But village kids are often responsible for that sort of thing."

Mrs. Quinn was just coming up from the kitchens as Kristy and Michael came into the rear of the courtyard. She carried a market basket on her arm and was dressed in a dark coat with a shawl thrown over her head. Obviously, she was heading for the village.

"Is Ned still asleep?" Kristy inquired, remembering her responsibility as baby-sitter.

The cook smiled and nodded. "Not a word have we heard from the little angel," she assured Kristy. "But you might look in on him. Nora has just gone down for her rest."

Kristy took Michael's coat and hung it in the hall closet, then excused herself. She tiptoed up the stairs to Ned's room, hoping to find him still fast asleep and thereby gain a little more time to spend with Michael alone.

Opening the bedroom door softly, she glanced inside, then started forward. The comforter was thrown back and the bed was empty. Suddenly the castle seemed preternaturally quiet. "Ned!" Kristy called. "Ned, where are you? Come here at once!"

Silence answered. Kristy ran across the room and flung open the closet door, then dropped to her knees and peered under the bed. "Ned!" she called again, fruitlessly, then pounded downstairs to the basement and along the service hall to Nora's room.

Knocking on the door, she called, "Nora, is Ned with you?" hoping she didn't sound as frantic as she felt.

A flannel wrapper clutched around her shoulders, Nora

appeared in an instant. "No, Miss Kristy. Isn't he still asleep?"

Kristy shook her head. "He isn't in his room." Then panic swept her. "He must be hiding. He can't be gone!"

Racing back upstairs she alerted Michael and together they ran through the castle, opening every closed door, searching every cupboard and closet, while shouting Ned's name at the top of their lungs.

In less than five minutes Nora joined them, dressed in her uniform once more. "Could he have slipped outside?" she asked, and ran across the courtyard without a coat, peering into the stables, trying the locked garage door.

"I doubt it," Kristy called back. "Mrs. Quinn just left for the village. She would have seen him."

"I'll try the O'Malleys'," Nora told Kristy. "He loves to play with the children. He may have trotted down there."

Not a sign had Mrs. O'Malley seen of the child, however, although she was as concerned as if it had been one of her own who was lost. She and Rosaleen and Dagan, the eldest boy, joined in the search, but after half an hour of scouring the grounds and once more scrutinizing every nook and cranny in the castle, the verdict was inescapable.

Unbelievable as it seemed, Ned had truly disappeared.

13

Kristy didn't cry, although she did something quite as uncharacteristic. She stood wringing her hands, while a feeling of desperation convulsed her throat.

Everyone, she realized, was thinking of the river, although no one spoke of it. Michael had already gone down to the sheep pasture, and could be seen in the distance running along the grassy bank toward the bridge. "We've got to *do* something," she cried distractedly. "We've got to send out an alarm."

For the first time she was expected to act as an adult must in an adult world. She was the responsible party, and it was up to her to make the next move. Aunt Irene would have called the guards before this, she realized, and consequently hurried inside.

As usual, Miss Bessie Donovan answered promptly, not

with the conventional "Number please?" but with a cheery acknowledgment that she liked to talk with the castle. "Good afternoon. What can I do for you today?"

Her geniality deserved a pleasant reply, but Kristy's alarm made her brusque. "I don't have the number, Miss Donovan, but can you connect me with the *gardai?* It's an emergency!"

"This is Miss Kristy, isn't it?" asked the postmistress perspicaciously.

"Yes."

"What's happened? Something else connected with Fergus O'Malley, I'll be bound." Bessie Donovan led a lonely life, and every tidbit of news was important to her.

"Please hurry!" Kristy begged, then added impatiently, "This has nothing to do with Fergus. My little cousin Ned has disappeared."

"Ned? You mean the three-year-old? Oh, my, that's terrible!" There was a clicking sound on the wire. "Wait a minute. Hang on, dear. The line is busy right now."

"I'm here," Kristy said, feeling as though she were going to choke.

"Where's the rest of the family?"

"Off on a sightseeing trip."

"I suppose you've looked everywhere?"

"Everywhere," Kristy replied. She supposed they would drag the river. If Ned had been drowned she would never forgive herself, never! Her flesh crawled and she wondered how she could possibly break the news to her aunt and uncle. Sinking down to a stool by the telephone table, she sat hunched forward with her elbows on her knees and her eyes closed while she tried to collect herself.

"Still busy," Miss Donovan said. "I was just thinking, is the tinker still camped across the road?"

"No. They left about an hour ago." Kristy answered automatically, but her mind was racing. Ned had been so fascinated by the gypsy child. He had kept looking back wistfully as she led him home. And Ned was a tenacious little boy, who clung to an idea much longer than most children his age. "But surely the gypsies wouldn't make off with him?" she asked, scarcely aware that she had spoken her thought aloud.

"Not deliberately, I shouldn't think," said Miss Donovan as though she, too, were considering the possibility. "Though they do say the Romany folk have a special fondness for little ones. A gypsy woman never balks at raising children who aren't her own."

Kristy came to a sudden decision. "When you reach the *gardai*, please tell them Ned is missing, and ask them to get over here as soon as possible. His parents may be home any minute, and they'll be frantic. I'll try to find the gypsies, somehow or other, just in case." She hung up without thinking to say good-bye, and went hurrying back outdoors.

Michael, breathless and increasingly concerned, came

running along the drive to where Nora and Mrs. O'Malley were consulting together. "No trace of him," he called. "You'd better ring up the *gardai.*"

"I already have," said Kristy. "Michael, there's a chance—just a chance!—that he might have gone off with the gypsies. We know, roughly, which direction they went. Do you think we could catch up with them?"

"The gypsies? Why the gypsies? What have they got to do with Ned?"

"I'll tell you on the way. Just let's get going!" Kristy's need for action was imperative. She was already mounting Nora's bicycle, without even a by-your-leave.

Michael could do nothing but follow. Kristy coasted downhill and crossed the bridge, then looked in dismay at the roads converging at the "Wiley Salmon." One led straight uphill to the snow-clad Nagles Mountains, another turned left along the Blackwater toward Fermoy, and the third turned right toward Convamore and Killavullen.

"They couldn't have gone toward Convamore," said Michael at once. "We'd have seen the wagon across the river as we went through the garden to the boathouse."

"Where does the uphill road lead?"

"Straight over the mountains, then down toward Cork."

"It would be hard on the horse to pull a wagon up that grade," said Kristy. "Let's try the river road to Fermoy."

193

Michael agreed. Standing on the pedals, the pair pumped as fast as they could, jouncing along the narrow, curving strip of macadam, pockmarked and scarred with age and use. They passed a cluster of cottages, a church, a farmhouse or two, then emerged on a level stretch leading through fields protected by thorn hedges. Far in the distance, across the river, Kristy could see the stark Georgian facade of Castle Hyde, sitting in all its matronly elegance on a carpet of green grass.

A lane, bordered by wispy trees and a tangle of vines, led through the fields to the river. Near its banks Kristy saw a glint of yellow, a streak of red, which could be a patch of gorse that kept its color even in December in this southern county. A few protected geraniums might still be clinging to a wall. She braked and looked more intently down the lane, then shouted to Michael, who had gone on ahead.

When he had turned around and pulled up beside her she said, "Could that be the wagon, or am I imagining things?"

"Let's have a look," Michael said at once. Parking their bikes against a tree, they went skidding and slipping along the muddy path, and came to a gate leading into a small abandoned farmyard. The former farmhouse was no more than a shack, but to Kristy and Michael this was of no importance, for its crumbling walls hid the tinker's wagon they were searching for.

194

Apparently the gypsies had just arrived. The horse was still standing in the wagon shafts, and the woman was fetching river water in a bucket, while her husband dragged some damp firewood into the shelter of a spreading holly tree.

Both stopped work in surprise as Kristy and Michael slogged across the mire toward them. At this crucial moment, their objective reached, it dawned on the pair that this was probably a wild-goose chase. Tongue-tied, they stared at each another. Then Kristy burst out, "The little boy—the one who was with me this morning—have you seen him anywhere?"

The tinker answered for his wife. Shaking his head, he asked, "What makes you think we should have seen him, missy?" There was a hint of truculence in his voice.

"Because he's lost," Kristy explained. "He must have wandered away. And he just loved your baby, remember?" She turned appealingly toward the woman and stretched out her hands, palms upward. "I thought perhaps he might have come back to you."

The gypsy drew herself up, and in spite of her tawdry earrings and unkempt hair she suddenly acquired stature. "We are not baby stealers," she said with unexpected dignity. "We are not kidnappers."

"I'm sorry," Kristy apologized. "We've been so terribly upset." Tears of anxiety welled up in her eyes. "Surely you can understand."

Michael was less ready to accept the gypsy's statement at face value. "You won't object if we take a look in the wagon," he said to the tinker. As he spoke he moved to the back of the vanlike cart and high-handedly pulled the door open, while the gypsy woman cautioned, "Careful there! My baby's asleep inside."

"Michael, please!" Kristy was embarrassed, and anxious to get away.

"Wait!" Michael's voice, usually so gentle, was as sharp as a pistol shot. He pulled down the stepladder that led to the rear of the wagon, mounting it in a flash. Kristy and the gypsies, moving closer, were in time to see him take a pencil flashlight from his hip pocket and play the slender beam over the interior. The corners were piled high with quilts and tattered blankets, and cook pots hung from the roof. Near the rear lay two plump gunnysacks from which wilted leaves protruded, and on one of them, cuddled together like puppies, lay a pair of sleeping forms.

"Ned!" Kristy's shout would have raised the dead, let alone a three-year-old. She crowded into the wagon beside Michael, gathered her young cousin into her arms, and rocked him maternally, while he yawned and grumbled and tried vainly to wake up.

The gypsy baby, on the other hand, came from sleep to full consciousness with the speed of a thunderbolt. And the instant he was awake he crawled toward his mother, who was standing, trancelike, without moving a muscle.

196

The tinker, staring at Ned as though he were an apparition, was the first to speak. "What's all this?" he muttered, turning to his wife. "How did he get there?"

"I don't know." She backed off a few steps, looking warily from her husband to Michael. Her eyes were both fearful and crafty, but there was a quality in her voice that made Kristy believe her. Smoothing the damp hair back from Ned's forehead, Kristy said, "I think she's telling the truth."

"Missy, believe me, I am!" The gypsy came back toward the wagon, and for a few seconds Kristy was afraid she might drop down to her knees in the mud, in an extravagant gesture of supplication.

Michael forestalled her. Accusingly, he said. "You're trying to claim you didn't make off with this child?"

"As God is my witness, I didn't know he was there!" The woman's voice rose to a shriek of protestation.

"Sh!" Kristy cautioned. "Let me ask Ned what happened." She sat the child on the floorboards by her side, and tried to rouse him. "Ned, how did you get in the wagon? Did the gypsy lady put you there?"

A beatific smile crossed Ned's face as he shook his head vigorously. "I climb the steps," he said.

"All by yourself?" Kristy asked.

Ned nodded.

"Why?" pursued Kristy, although she anticipated the answer.

"To play with the baby."

"But the baby was frightened of you. He would have screamed."

Ned shook his head again. "Baby asleep."

This made sense to Kristy. "So you went to sleep too."

"I took my nap." Ned agreed with a smile.

"But how did you get out of the castle?"

The question seemed to surprise the child. "Walk."

"By yourself?"

"Yes," Ned said proudly. "Myself."

"That was very naughty of you," Kristy scolded. "You must never go out of the house without a grown-up. You see what happened. You got lost."

"I'm not lost," Ned objected, and the gypsies laughed spontaneously. No doubt they thought the danger of being accused of kidnapping was over, but Michael was still suspicious.

"It seems very strange that neither one of you spotted the child in the wagon," he said to the tinker and his wife. "I very much doubt that the *gardai* would accept Ned's explanation. You could be in real trouble if they caught wind of this affair."

The gypsies obviously thought so too. Apparently they lived with the *gardai* in a state of uneasy truce. If they kept out of trouble, they were allowed to camp along the country roads and ply their trade, but at the first hint of questionable behavior they were denied their age-old squatters' rights and were moved along unceremoniously.

Kristy, although she was aware that Michael's veiled threat might be justified, was still inclined to give this swarthy couple the benefit of the doubt. After all, Ned was safe and sound. Besides, his explanation held water. The excursion on which he had evidently started while she and Michael were lunching, and while Nora thought he was safely asleep, was completely in character.

"Come on, Michael, please!" she urged to avoid any further discussion. "We've got to get Ned back home. My uncle and aunt will be utterly frantic!"

The prospect of going home didn't please Ned in the least. He had come to play with the baby and now Kristy's friend was swinging him up to his shoulders and carrying him off. In contrast to his reaction that morning, the gypsy baby peered from the rear of the wagon, quite self-contained, while now Ned bawled at the top of his lungs as he was carried arbitrarily along the lane.

However, the chance to ride on the handlebars of Michael's bicycle soon mollified him. His tears stopped abruptly, and by the time they glimpsed the bridge across the Blackwater at a turn in the road, he was completely enamored of his new mode of locomotion.

Michael, on the other hand, was puffing and straining on each slight grade. "This child weighs a ton," he complained to Kristy. "Maybe we should have made the tinker bring him back in the wagon instead of carting him off ourselves."

"I think you were sort of mean to those gypsies," Kristy took the opportunity to remark. "Knowing this young imp as well as I do by now, I'll bet it all happened just the way he said."

"Possibly—even probably," agreed Michael equably, "but on the other hand the tinkers are a devious tribe. Often, they're drifters and vagabonds, and accustomed to living by their wits."

Kristy let the subject drop. She reminded herself that she had every reason to be grateful to Michael. After all, it was he who had taken matters into his own hands and flung open the door of the wagon. He, not she, had found Ned, and he had a right to a hero's welcome at the castle. She was only sorry their return couldn't be more dramatic. Instead of riding Ned home on his handlebars, Michael should have been able to carry him triumphantly into the hall on a shield.

The white, midwinter twilight was reflected in the windows of Ballyhooly as the bicyclists reached the bridge. Dismounting at the foot of the steep hill, Kristy walked ahead on the way to the top. Mrs. O'Malley, the first person to see them turn into the park, came running to greet them.

"Glory be to God!" she cried. "If it isn't the little one! Where had he got to, the precious lamb?"

Suddenly Kristy and Michael were surrounded. Aunt Irene, tears of relief streaming down her cheeks, came flying down the drive to hug her young son to her, while Nora, Mrs. Quinn, and the Hendersons came hurrying along behind. Two young men from the *gardai*, strangers to Kristy, joined the group, and everyone asked questions at once.

"Michael found him!" Kristy explained proudly, and parried the questions thrust at her with happy retorts. As everyone moved toward the castle courtyard, where two *gardai* cars were pulled up beside the family's, she ventured a question of her own.

"Where's Uncle Robert? Off somewhere looking for Ned? He ought to be told!"

A pall of constraint settled on the adults. "He's inside talking to Superintendent Kelly," Kristy's father explained finally. "But you're quite right, Kristy. I'll go tell him at once that Ned's safe."

Michael stood by his bike, making a tentative effort to say good-bye. "Nonsense," said Kristy's grandmother when she discovered his intention. "You must stay for dinner. As a matter of fact, why not stay the night? We've plenty of room, and I don't like the thought of having you travel that narrow road in the dark."

"My aunt is expecting me," Michael demurred, but not vigorously.

"Telephone her," Kristy suggested.

"I'll play you a game of chess," Sam offered as though this should clinch the bargain.

"It's very kind of you, Mrs. Henderson," Michael said to Kristy's grandmother. "If you're sure I won't be in the way—"

At this moment, erupting from the main door like a jet-borne projectile, came Superintendent Kelly. Bluff, red-faced, and pompous, he seemed unusually pleased with himself. "I must ask you all to accompany me to the drawing room," he said with a cursory glance at Ned, to whom he seemed to attach no more importance than one might to a rescued puppy. He held the door back with one hand and barked, "At once, if you please."

Concerned by the officer's peremptory manner, the Hendersons trailed in, Kristy's grandparents first, then her parents. Sam, unexpectedly courteous, waited for Aunt Irene and Ned to precede him. Kristy and Michael brought up the rear.

The two young *gardai*, apparently uncertain whether to go or stay, came along behind; their job was over, and they were obviously anxious to be gone. Nora and Mrs. Quinn went off in the direction of the kitchens, while Mary stood in the hall and beamed at Ned and his mother as they passed by.

"What's up, do you suppose?" Kristy asked Michael in an undertone.

Michael's shoulders twitched in a slight shrug. "I haven't a clue."

202

If the superintendent overhead the exchange, he ignored it. The last to enter the crowded room, he shut the door after him, then looked around as though something were amiss. His eye lighted on the two *gardai*, standing uncomfortably side by side near the bookcases. "You may be excused, lads," he said. "I'm sure you have more important things to do."

Kristy scarcely noticed the young men leave. Her attention was focused on her Uncle Robert, who had hurried over and taken Ned from his wife's arms. He seemed to take comfort in holding his son, patting him on the back as Superintendent Kelly took up a stance before the fireplace.

"If you will all be seated, please."

Uncle Robert was the last to sit down, and instead of sinking into the easy chair he had long since appropriated as the spot affording the best reading light, he let himself down on a stiff side chair and placed Ned on the floor between his knees. Restless, the child tried to break away, but his father held him fast, as though he were clinging to the sturdy little body for support. Kristy was aware that her uncle looked unusually pale and that his eyes were dark and perplexed.

"It is my duty," boomed the superintendent, rocking back and forth on his heels within inches of the fire in the grate, "to tell you that the laboratory report is now complete. The poison contained in the can placed by Mr.

Russell on the wardrobe shelf in Mr. Henderson's bed-room is identical to that discovered in the stomach and lungs of Fergus O'Malley, deceased.

"Mr. Russell, I arrest you in the name of the law."

14

There was a moment's shocked silence. Then Kristy's grandmother jumped to her feet. "But that's insane!" she cried, no more afraid of the superintendent than if he had been an especially annoying fly invading the drawing room. "My son-in-law explained where he found the can, and why he put it where he did."

"I regret, madam, that I have no other recourse. Mr. Russell must accompany me to Cork, where he will be interrogated by our criminal investigators. In due course it may be possible to arrange bail."

"What's due course?" Sam asked his mother, who said "Sh!" and frowned at her husband, as though entreating him to back Grandma up.

Uncle Robert, at this point, put Ned aside and stood up. "I'm afraid there's no use arguing," he said as though he had been over this same ground earlier. "Suppose you come along later, Steve, and see if you can't spring me. I have no special desire to spend a night in an Irish jail."

"I'd better pack a small bag for you, just in case," said Aunt Irene with astonishing composure. "You'll need a toothbrush and your shaving things."

She left the room, followed by Uncle Robert and the superintendent. Immediately, Kristy's grandmother whirled on her husband. "For goodness sake," she cried accusingly, "can't you *do* anything?"

"I'm afraid there's nothing to do, dear." Kristy could sense the distress only half concealed by her grandfather's deliberately mild tone of voice. "As Robert says, we can probably post bail later."

"But it's all so idiotic!" Grandma fumed.

"From our point of view, yes," Kristy's mother agreed. "But I suppose the guards are within their rights, considering the circumstantial evidence." She looked at her husband questioningly. "I'll go with you, and probably Irene will want to come along too."

"Can I come?" asked Sam, endlessly eager for adventure.

"You may not," replied his mother, correcting his grammar even in this time of stress. "You need a good night's sleep."

"And so do the old folks," said Grandma, suddenly deflated. "It's been a long, hard day!"

Grandpa came over and put his arm around her. "We'll curl up under our electric blankets right after dinner and let the young people cope."

"Cope?" Kristy wailed softly. "But nobody's coping! We're simply standing around while poor Uncle Robert is being marched off to jail!" She wanted to go with him, to try to help, but the term young people, she realized, actually referred to the middle-aged. She and Michael were not to be included. They'd probably be forced to spend a long and unprofitable evening entertaining Sam.

Kristy had reckoned without gauging the effect of a day of fresh air on an active eleven-year-old boy. Sam was still full of bounce when he set up the chessboard, but by the time he and Michael had reached the middle game he was beginning to yawn.

A deliberate and careful player, Michael continued to take his time. Meanwhile Kristy grew increasingly restless. She paced the room, poked up the fire, then spotted the scotch tape she had bought several days ago. Now would be as good a time as any to fasten the pages about Ballyhooly's Ghostly Catch back in the book.

A question still baffled her. What possible reason could Fergus have had for secreting the torn pages in his bedroom? In reading the story herself, could she possibly have overlooked a clue?

With the pages taped securely in place once more, Kristy curled up on the sofa and began to reread the story as the chess game dragged on.

Ned was asleep; Mary had turned down the beds and left for home; Mrs. Quinn's son had called for her in a ramshackle car that taxied her back and forth night and morning. Grandpa and Grandma, true to their promise, had retired early, and Nora was presumably in her room on the ground floor.

Kristy herself began to feel sleepy, but she persevered. The tale was just as she had remembered it, and although she read through to the end, there were no surprises. Then a footnote at the bottom of the last page caught her eye. By nature Kristy was allergic to footnotes. They seemed unnecessarily pedantic and usually bored her, but the word "spurge" almost leaped from the small type and gave her pause.

"One should remember that these are legends and not local histories, although some have a core of historic truth," Kristy read. "It may be that poachers, using crushed spurge as a narcotic, managed to anesthetize a large haul of fish, although not in the quantities described."

The footnote bore out Aunt Irene's conviction that there was often a kernel of fact in these old ghost stories. It also occurred to Kristy that Fergus might have got an interesting idea from this note. She wanted to talk to

Michael, but without Sam as a kibitzer. "Can't you hurry things up?" she asked the chess players. "Or is this going to take all night?"

Neither answered, but a minute later Michael made a foolish move and Sam quickly checkmated him. By now he was so sleepy he didn't even wait to gloat, but swept the chessmen into their box and trotted off to bed without any objection at all.

"Was that a calculated misplay?" Kristy asked when her brother had left the room.

"How did you guess?" returned Michael, who was standing by the fire, stretching. "Sam could probably have beaten me anyway. The boy's really good."

Kristy, book in hand, came over and sat down on the hearth rug, while Michael lowered himself beside her and said with a sigh of relief, "It's nice to be alone."

Kristy nodded. "Read this," she said, holding out the book, "and see what you make of it. Not the whole story, just the footnote. You remember I told you that Rosaleen found the torn pages in Fergus's room."

Michael nodded, holding the book close to the firelight so that he could read the fine print. When he had finished he glanced up at Kristy and gave a low whistle. "He was sure interested in poaching techniques, wasn't he? It's odd that you should show me this just now, because I've been thinking about those gypsies. Actually, I believe you're right that they didn't carry Ned off deliberately.

The tinker looked too astonished, but there was something shifty about that pair, nevertheless. They acted scared of being trapped."

Kristy agreed.

"And why would they choose to camp in such a remote spot? Nobody's going to go past there with pots or pans to mend."

"I hadn't thought of that," Kristy said, although she couldn't guess where the conversation was leading.

"There's another thing," Michael continued. "When I opened the wagon door I caught a whiff of something I couldn't put a name to. Remember those gunnysacks the children were sleeping on, Kristy? I'm pretty sure I know what they were filled with, and it certainly wasn't straw."

"What was it?"

"Spurge."

"Spurge?" Kristy clapped her hands ecstatically. "Oh, Michael, it begins to fit! The gypsies picked up the sacks from the slope above the graveyard and they're delivering it to the poachers at their hideaway. I'll bet the headquarters is that abandoned farmhouse!" Her eyes sparkled and she no longer felt sleepy. "If only we could trap them there!"

"Wow!" Michael said. "You do leap to conclusions!"

"But you said yourself that if we could find the spurge we'd be in possession of an important clue!"

"You're putting words into my mouth," Michael protested, "but I agree that it would be a step forward. Now if we could catch Liam McMurrough red-handed he might break down and give the rest of the gang away."

"Michael?"

"Yes?"

"Do you think Liam could have killed Fergus?" Kristy put the question tentatively, as though the thought was too dreadful to entertain.

"There's no telling," Michael replied. "At least at this point. We know they had a fight and that Liam moved out of the tower, but we don't know what happened after that."

"I wish we knew where he's living. Could it possibly be that farmhouse?"

"Say, that's an idea! I wonder who owns the place? I could ask my aunt."

"Phone her now!" urged Kristy, "while I go check on Sam. After my experience with Ned, I'm running scared."

Michael picked up the receiver and gave the Fermoy number to Miss Donovan as Kristy slipped out of the room. The hall was chilly, as usual, and she wasted no time in getting to Sam's room. When she opened the bedroom door she could hear his regular breathing, but even so she went inside to make sure he was well covered. As she bent over the bed she happened to glance upward. With a stifled gasp she straightened and peered out of the

211

window. There was a light in the castle tower, just as there had been on Christmas eve! The ghost of Ballyhooly must be walking again!

Afterward, Kristy could not have estimated how long she stayed in the room. Time stood still, for a space that might have covered one minute or ten, as she watched the peripatetic, lurid beam, lighting first one narrow aperture, then another.

The sight was shocking because it was so inexplicable. Who could be prowling the ramparts or searching the dusty rooms? Was it Liam McMurrough, still trying to find the poison that had caused Uncle Robert's arrest? Was it the ghost the gypsy fortune-teller had described so effectively? Or could it be the shade of Fergus O'Malley, consigned to a poacher's purgatory until the mystery of his strange death was cleared?

Kristy was frightened. Her hands were clammy, her forehead damp, her eyes huge with foreboding. Finally, she turned and on tiptoe retraced her steps, closing the door of Sam's room softly. Then she tore along the dark hall as though banshees were after her, as indeed they might be.

"Michael!" she cried, bursting into the drawing room. "There's a light in the tower again!" She went into his arms like a terrified child and he caught her close for a moment, then held her off by the shoulders.

"Are you sure?"

Kristy's teeth were chattering but she managed to breathe, "Oh, yes!"

Roughly, Michael shook her. "Certainly, at your age, you don't believe in ghosts?"

"Then who could it be?"

"McMurrough, most likely. Kristy, here's our chance!"

"Our chance for what? You're not going near there?" Kristy clung to him, but Michael pulled away.

"Don't be such a scaredy-cat!"

The childish admonishment brought Kristy to her senses in an instant. "All right," she said without a trace of her former hysteria. "If you're going, I'm going too."

"Can you see the castle entrance from the tower windows?" asked Michael as they gathered up their coats from a hall chair.

Kristy shook her head, but even so she turned off the overhead light, then felt her way to the courtyard in Michael's wake, closing the heavy door silently. The stones underfoot were slippery and black, the night air frosty. Bare trees reached out branches like arms toward the rising tower, almost invisible, a relic of bygone days when ghouls peopled the stories told in the pubs and ghosts were as real as death or taxes to the country folk.

City-bred, Michael was a realist. He could see the light in the tower as well as Kristy, but that it could be superhuman he found absurd. Even though he didn't speak, clearly the only thought in his mind was how to capture

213

the intruder. Creeping along the wall, he reached a place opposite the door, which was ajar, then waited for Kristy.

"If only there was a moon—" he whispered.

"There is, but it's behind the clouds," Kristy whispered back. "Besides, if we could see better, we could also be seen."

This remark led Michael to take stock of their position. "If the prowler flashes his torch as he comes through that door, we'll be pinned against the wall in its light."

"That's dangerous."

"You bet it is!" Michael agreed. "I'm a fair enough wrestler in my own weight group, but I'd be no match for a husky country fellow."

"Maybe we can lock him in?" Kristy proposed

"Provided he's left the key in the lock. Can you see?"

"I couldn't see a white cat three feet in front of me," Kristy whispered back. "Anyway, the key is huge, and you have to fiddle with it." She was remembering Fergus O'Malley opening the door for the family that first day. It had taken him fully thirty seconds to turn the lock after he had pulled back the bar.

"The bar!" Kristy clutched Michael's arm. "There's a big bar. We won't need a key at all."

This knowledge provided Michael with new courage. "We've got to move now, and move fast!"

Michael changed to a crouching position, preparing to sprint across the courtyard. "You'd better stay here," he said at the last moment, but Kristy ignored the warning and followed, running as silently as she could. From the tower came the ominous creak of the rickety stair treads, making her skin prickle. Would they be too late?

Reaching the half-open door a second before Kristy, Michael slammed it shut and leaned against it as he felt for the bar. From within came a man's throaty curse, the shock of a heavy body heaving against the oaken panels, just as the bolt slid home.

Kristy's knees felt weak. She leaned against the tower wall and asked a foolish question, "Do you think it will hold?"

Michael had taken out his pencil flashlight and was playing it over the blackened wood with its heavy iron fittings. "I'd say it would hold until kingdom come," he replied, still breathless. "If it's held prisoners safe since Cromwellian times, I don't think we have a thing to worry about."

Inside, their captive was battering futiley at the barred door. Kristy wished she could shout, "You may as well give up!" but she was afraid of awakening Ned and Nora, whose bedrooms were on this side of the house. "I wish we could find out if it's Liam McMurrough," she said to Michael, then had a bright idea as the pounding ceased and the tower was quiet once more.

She seized Michael's flashlight and skirted the wall until she reasoned that she must have reached the point below the window on the first floor landing. The aperture wasn't visible, but her memory for detail was keen and her estimate was shrewd. Suddenly she shone the torch upward, and was rewarded by the fleeting glimpse of a red-bearded face behind the rusted bars.

The man was a total stranger, and for a moment disappointment overwhelmed her. She had been so sure that Liam was the culprit that she had fully expected to see his scarred and swarthy countenance. "It's nobody we know!" she said in an undertone to Michael. "Did you see? He has red hair and a red beard!"

Michael shook his head. He hadn't been as quick-eyed as Kristy. "Is there any other way out of the tower?" he asked.

"No," replied Kristy confidently. "The window slits are too narrow to slide through. Besides, even the one on the landing must be fifteen feet above ground."

She had barely finished speaking when automobile tires crunched on the graveled drive and headlights swept along the garden wall. "They're home!" Kristy cried softly as she started toward the garage area. "Oh, good! The family is home."

The four adults who had been jacknifed into the small car got out and stretched tentatively, as though they could scarcely believe their good fortune in being back at the castle again. Kristy breathed a quick sigh of relief when she recognized her Uncle Robert among them, and mentally applauded the family's success in getting him released from spending a night in the Cork jail.

Appearing out of the darkness with Michael at her side, Kristy came as a shock to her parents. "What are you doing here at this time of night?" her father asked.

"You'll never guess—" Kristy started, but Michael stepped forward and interrupted. "We've just captured a prowler, sir. We've got him locked in the tower." His tone was more boyish than usual, and not without pride.

Kristy's mother pretended to stagger, and leaned against the front fender. "Oh, no!" she groaned. "I can't believe it, and I won't. Not all in one day!"

"He's quite safe, ma'am. He can't get out," Michael said soothingly.

"I saw his face," Kristy told everyone. "Just for a second. At the window. It's nobody I've ever seen before."

"Now what do we do?" asked Aunt Irene. "I think it would be just jolly to call the guards again."

"Jolly or not, that's what we'd better do," decided Uncle Robert. "Can't you imagine the uproar if we take the law into our own hands and keep this fellow here all night?"

Kristy's mother yawned audibly. "I am not for Women's Lib," she said. "I claim my rights as a weak and weary female, and I suggest that you do the same, Irene. You men take care of things. I'm going to bed."

And to bed she went, although Aunt Irene didn't fol-

217

low. She joined the others in the drawing room, where Kristy's father, still bundled into his warm tweed topcoat, had hurried to the telephone.

"Miss Donovan," he said, "I'm terribly sorry to disturb you at this late hour, but I'll have to ask you to ring the *gardai* in Fermoy."

The reply on the other end of the line erupted in the room like static. Stephen Henderson, with a wry grin, held the receiver away from his ear and waited. "Nothing is wrong with the family, Miss Donovan," he said after an interval. "Everyone is here and accounted for." He put his hand over the mouthpiece and glanced at Kristy. "I hope!"

Kristy nodded, and again came a crackling sound. "We are *all* here," her father said rather brusquely, and Uncle Robert stepped forward and made a mock bow.

The room was silent for a few seconds. Then came the echo of a ring, followed quickly by an audible voice. "Fermoy *gardai*, Sergeant Walsh here."

Aunt Irene shut her eyes and moaned plaintively. "Not Sergeant Walsh again!"

"This is Stephen Henderson, calling from Ballyhooly," said Kristy's father, knowing that of course Miss Donovan was listening in. "We have captured a prowler and locked him in the tower." (In an aside to Michael he explained that he was using the editorial *we*.) "No, we don't know who it is. . . . Yes, my daughter saw his face for an instant.

218

She says he has a red beard. . . . Quite safe, I can assure you. As you know, the tower windows are very narrow, and even a skinny child would have trouble slipping through."

A fresh volley of crackling sound came from the other end of the line. Stephen Henderson pushed forward his lower lip, while his eyes brightened in amusement. He kept nodding and saying "Hmm," then flashed a glance around the room. "I quite agree," he said at last. "I *quite* agree! He may be uncomfortable, but he can't possibly freeze."

Another pause followed, while Sergeant Walsh spoke and Kristy's father listened. "In the morning then," he replied. "Shall we say nine-thirty? It would be nice to have a quiet breakfast, and the maids don't serve until nine."

This disposition of the prowler seemed rather high-handed to Kristy and Michael. They looked at each another, aghast, but Aunt Irene applauded. "Good for you, Steve!" she cried as her brother hung up. "I think it's high time we stood on our rights!"

15

A rooster crowed, out of tune with the key of the morning wind, which was light and bitter. Dawn, for the last time before the year's end, moved along the rim of the mountains. Down in the valley Kristy could hear an early cart rattling over the bridge. She lay in bed, hands clasped behind her head, waiting for the day to begin.

There was a knock at the door, then a whisper. "Kristy, are you awake?"

"Michael! Yes. Why?"

"Get up and get dressed, quickly. I've got an idea."

Kristy pulled on slacks, a shirt, and a warm sweater, without turning on a light. The thin pink streaks in the gunmetal sky had broadened only slightly by the time she tiptoed into the hall.

Michael was standing close to the main door, a woolen

cap covering his curly hair, a scarf around his throat. He put a finger to his lips to forestall Kristy's question and held her coat while she slipped her arms into the sleeves. Then he led her quietly outside and across the courtyard to the garage area, where the bikes were parked.

Not until they were out of sight of the living quarters did Michael speak. "Last night," he said, "I never got a chance to tell you about the conversation with Aunt Sheila. Do you know who owns that property where the gypsies were camping? Mrs. Quinn."

"You mean the cook?"

Michael nodded. "Furthermore, she's Liam McMurrough's godmother."

"So what?" Kristy stood shivering in the half-light, waiting for Michael to get to the point.

"So it's more than likely she felt sorry for the bloke when Fergus kicked him out of the tower. What would be more natural than to let him move into that tumbledown shack if he needed a place to sleep?"

"But Mrs. Quinn is such a *nice* woman," Kristy protested.

"Of course she's a nice woman, but she's also Liam's godmother, and she's bound to feel a certain responsibility."

Growing chillier by the minute, Kristy hugged her elbows with her gloved hands. "We could go ask her, I suppose," she suggested, spurred by the thought of the

warm and steamy kitchen, where preparations for breakfast must be getting under way.

Michael shook his head. "There isn't time. The villagers are already stirring, and an hour from now all of
Ballyhooly and most of Fermoy will know about that
telephone conversation with my aunt." Michael lifted his
bike across the crushed-stone drive and set it down on the
frosty grass. "They'll also know we have a captive in the
tower, you can depend on that!"

"But how?" Kristy asked.

"Miss Bessie isn't one to let grass grow under her feet,"
replied Michael. "There hasn't been so much excitement
around here since a Blackwater gillie won the sweep-
stakes."

"The salmon season opens day after tomorrow," Michael continued. "The fish have been traveling upstream
for some time now, and a good many must be resting in
this reach of the river. Any poacher knows that when the
sports fishermen arrive, and the gillies launch the boats,
his chance of a big haul is over. So if spurge is being used
by Liam or anyone else, you can bet it's in the water right
now!"

"O.K. Let's go!" Kristy took Nora's bicycle from the
rack and copied Michael's maneuver. Silently, keeping to
the grass, they approached the gate, lifted the bikes over
the cattle guard, then mounted and coasted rapidly downhill and across the bridge.

Kristy looked back once, wondering if they could be spotted from the castle, but in the half-light Michael looked like any laborer on his way to work, and she could have been a shopgirl bound for Fermoy.

Michael turned quickly into the river road, and Kristy breathlessly followed. Whipped by the moist wind to scarlet, her cheeks burned with the cold, but she didn't complain. Every minute counted, if they were to reach the farmhouse before full daylight, when presumably a poacher would not take the unnecessary risk of being seen and caught.

From a break in a stone wall came a mongrel dog, yapping at Kristy's heels. She stood on the pedals and pumped harder, glancing up at the country church when she passed it, and trying to reckon the remaining distance to the lane. The dog gave up and trotted off, his attention diverted by a dead fox lying at the side of the road. Kristy, shuddering in distaste, kept her eyes ahead. If Michael had seen the fox, he gave no sign.

Smoke curled from the chimney of a cottage, but nobody was abroad. Michael braked and swung off his bike before Kristy was quite prepared. To the left she could barely make out the muddy path they had followed yesterday. It had been a quick trip.

Parking the bicycles against a tree well back from the main road, the pair kept to the right of the lane and crossed a stubbly field, screened from the gypsies' camp

223

by a border of tangled honeysuckle and thorn. Ahead the river coursed past Castle Hyde and there was little cover, so Michael detoured at the end of the lane and worked his way upstream.

Kristy followed, her boots heavy with mud, her toes frigid. She saw no sign of the painted wagon or its occupants, nor did a whiff of smoke indicate that anyone was stirring at the farm.

Fortunately, Michael knew every inch of the riverbank, where he had wandered on many a summer day. He drew Kristy into a small patch of woodland, then went cautiously forward, stepping carefully to avoid the crackling of twigs underfoot.

Kristy could now hear the faint splash of tumbling water, indicating that there must be a shallow falls nearby. Ahead, Michael stopped and waited for her to catch up, then grabbed her arm and silently pointed, mouthing the word "Look."

Taking shelter behind a thick tree trunk, Kristy craned forward. Below the falls a big salmon jumped wildly through a milky pool of water, then flopped around in a powerless struggle to breast the slight obstacle in the stream.

"Crushed spurge would make the water milky like that," Michael whispered. "The stuff knocks the fish out temporarily, but it doesn't kill them, you know."

Kristy didn't answer. Her attention had shifted to a

man with a long pole, standing close to the river at the edge of a narrow bit of bog.

His back was to them, but Kristy could see that he was a strapping, black-haired fellow. "Liam?" she whispered, her mouth close to Michael's ear.

"I think so."

Kristy watched while the man, who was wearing hip boots, waded into the water and spiked the salmon neatly, just behind the gills, depositing his illicit catch in a huge basket already brimming with fish. The mists and drifting fog of early morning made the scene unreal. The wind, creaking in the trees, was like a witch's lullaby, and the dawn seemed to tremble on the brink of day. "Ballyhooly's Ghostly Catch," Kristy breathed.

Suppose, she thought as she stood there, instead of a dearth of fish the salmon were really running, as they had in years past, hundreds of them fighting their way up the Blackwater to the spawning grounds. Not only the spring fish like these, weighing close to fifteen pounds, who had spent two years in the ocean, but the monsters of forty pounds returning after four years in the sea. A poacher would not be discriminating. He would take them all, the adolescent grilse and even the smolts along with the full salmon. Only those her father described as "rawners," the ugly reddish creatures that had failed to spawn, would be unsalable on the black market where he traded. Suddenly she hated this poacher—Liam McMurrough or whoever

225

he might be—with a fury that drove her forward. "Hey!" she was about to yell, when a hand was clamped over her mouth.

"Sh!" Michael's lips cautioned, holding her while she struggled for a moment, then subsided. "Don't be a fool," he whispered. "We've seen enough. We've got to get out of here."

As though he shared the same thought, the poacher turned, and in the gray light Kristy got a full look at his face. "It *is* Liam!" she whispered in turn.

Michael nodded, frowning. He seemed suddenly troubled. Perhaps he was regretting his impetuous decision to bring Kristy along on this risky jaunt.

As the morning sun, flickering through the clouds, turned the fish scales iridescent, Liam glanced up at the sky, then threw down his spiked pole and hoisted the heavy basket to his shoulder, staggering under its weight.

Michael pulled Kristy behind the tree once more, alarm making him incautious. She stumbled against him and a twig snapped sharply, making Liam swing around.

Crushed against the rough trunk and hidden by Michael's body, Kristy couldn't see what happened next. Her heart thudded against her chest and she scarcely dared breathe. If the poacher found them spying, they were in real danger. Liam hadn't earned that scar by walking away from a fight!

If only she had left a note for her parents! If only they

had some kind of weapon. Michael, as he had admitted last night, would never be a match for Liam, who was ten years older and twenty pounds heavier.

There was a thud, a grunt, and from Michael's heavy breathing Kristy sensed, rather than heard, McMurrough coming toward them. The copse of trees was a small one, the cover scant. Then came a muttered oath, followed by a rough, challenging voice.

"What do you think you're doing here?"

Moving away from Kristy and out into the open, Michael looked remarkably brave and belligerent. "What does it look like?"

"It don't look good," McMurrouch replied, his neck thrust forward. He took a couple of steps toward Michael and added, "What I'm aimin' to do to you ain't going to feel so good, either. I'll teach you to come snooping around my property!"

"It's not your property," contradicted Kristy, boldly stepping out from behind the tree. "It's Mrs. Quinn's."

For a split second the poacher was taken aback. He glanced from the boy to the girl just long enough for Michael to get in the first blow. This is what Kristy had hoped for, but the advantage she had gained was short-lived. McMurrough had a punch like a piston, and an inexperienced nineteen-year-old was no match for a ruffian who lived by no rules but his own.

Kristy could see that Michael was bound to be hurt,

227

and hurt badly. To stand helplessly by was unendurable, yet what could she do? To scream would be useless. Obviously, the gypsies had moved on, and there was no house within a quarter of a mile.

Suddenly an unexpected ally appeared. The feisty little dog who had followed Kristy down the road came racing through the stand of trees, yapping at the heels of the opponents. Liam kicked at the cur and missed, giving Michael a chance for another blow in the split second of inattention, but his fist merely grazed the poacher's jaw.

Liam punched Michael viciously in the face and the boy reeled backward. The dog yelped as a heel caught his foot and Kristy screamed, "Stop it, you big bully!"

She might as well have said, "Go to it, pal!" for all the effect the words had on McMurrough. A trickle of blood spilling from the corner of Michael's mouth seemed to whet his thirst for vengeance. Appearing to relish the thought of the power he was ready to unleash at any moment, he moved forward, step by slow step, as Michael backed away.

Kristy gasped, raised a hand to her mouth in an unconscious genture of horror, then glanced around frantically. The dog was limping off toward the river, and the fish were still flopping in the basket. Although only a few seconds had passed, she was surprised to find the landscape unchanged.

Then Kristy caught sight of the pike, lying where Liam

had dropped it. She was across the spongy ground in a flash, and as the poacher made a sudden leap and caught Michael in his brawny arms, wrestling him to the ground, she picked it up.

McMurrough's back was toward her. He was taking his time in knocking Michael out, apparently enjoying the fight and hating to bring it to an end. He didn't see Kristy come up behind him and raise the heavy pole into the air, but Michael, pinned beneath the man's body, suddenly found new courage, and his eyes held a glint of triumph.

With all her strength, Kristy brought the pole down on the back of McMurrough's skull. The whack, followed by Liam's groan, echoed in her ears. Then the poacher's body went limp, and he rolled over on the wet leaves, unconscious.

Michael was on his feet in an instant. "Bravo!" he cried, while Kristy, still clutching the fishing spear, stood looking down at the supine figure in consternation.

"Do—do you think I've killed him?" she breathed, appalled by her own action.

"Not Liam! He's got a hide like a rhinoceros. But you sure knocked him out!"

Kristy leaned the pike gingerly against the nearest tree trunk, handling it as though it was dangerous to relinquish but equally dangerous to hold. "What do we do now?" she asked. "Run?"

"Run? Are you kidding? It's something to catch a

poacher in the act. We've got to turn him over to the police."

"Michael, use some common sense! The minute he comes to we're in trouble again!"

Michael managed to grin in spite of his torn lip. "We'll tie him up!"

Kristy was still skeptical. "What with?"

"Give me the belt from your coat. It's strong, isn't it?"

"It's strong, but it's not long enough," said Kristy, unbuckling the belt and holding it out doubtfully.

"We'll join it to mine."

Fortunately both belts were leather. Michael buckled one to the other, then tested their combined strength. "Still not very long," he muttered. "Help me drag him over to that sapling, Kristy, and we'll see if we can make it reach."

Michael grabbed one of McMurrough's legs while Kristy conquered her feeling of repugnance and took hold of the other. "I don't trust that skinny tree trunk," she argued as they pulled the heavy body across the ground. "He could be strong enough to snap it right in half."

Then a new idea occurred to her. "Wait! He must have a belt of his own."

The three belts combined could girdle a stout oak, along with McMurrough's thick body, but because he was already stirring, Kristy and Michael had to work fast. They were breathing hard when they finally had him

230

pinioned, arms at his side, in a sitting position with his back against the rough bark.

"There!" Michael was trying to sound more satisfied with the job than he actually felt. "I'll stand guard while you get back to the castle, Kristy. Hurry as fast as you can, and for Pete's sake don't come back without the *gardai!*"

These orders made sense, but Kristy didn't underestimate the poacher's strength. She handed Michael the barbed pole. "Stand and hold those prongs against his throat till we get back," she commanded, "or I won't budge an inch."

Michael was amused by the fire in her eye, but he agreed willingly. "Would you go now?" he begged. "We're wasting time."

Kristy ran as fast as her mud-caked boots would allow, fear for Michael's safety spurring her on. The bicycles were standing where they had been left, and she mounted Nora's thankfully and started toward home. At once she realized that the return trip would be very slow going. Most of the road was uphill, and on the other side of the bridge the grade was so steep that she would be forced to dismount and walk. Weak-kneed with fright and exhaustion, she tried to stand on the pedals but collapsed back onto the seat within a few seconds. A fine courier she was making! It would have been wiser to send Michael to the castle and stay with McMurrough herself.

If only she could get to a telephone! However, Kristy

231

knew that not one of the coteens she was passing would boast such as instrument. There was only one directory for the whole of Ireland; country people could not afford the luxury of a telephone.

Not only Kristy's knees, but her arms began to tremble, and her breath came in short gasps. While she tried to convince herself that her exhaustion was only reaction setting in, she knew she was traveling at a snail's pace compared to her normal speed. A herd of sheep came bleating across the road, and she had to wait until they had reached a pasture gate, but the opportunity to catch her breath did little to refresh her.

The shepherd was a young boy, about Sam's age, nobody on whom she could call for help, and the next cluster of cottages had the closed look typical of all Irish houses in midwinter. A crane flew heavily toward the river and a rackety motor sounded in the distance. Kristy slipped down from the bike and stood staunchly in the middle of the pavement. If at all possible she intended to hitch a ride.

A light pickup truck came hurtling along the narrow road, then stopped with a squeal of brakes as a middle-aged man in a checkered cap leaned out the open window. "Hey, there! You want to get killed?"

Kristy shook her head. "I'm in trouble," she said. "Please give me a lift to Ballyhooly!"

"Got a flat tire?"

"No, it's much more serious than that. I'll explain on the way."

"Say, you're one of the Yanks from the castle, aren't you?" asked the man as he climbed obligingly down from the driver's seat and hoisted Nora's bicycle into the open rear. "Get in, young lady, if you can make it. Or do you need a hand up?"

Kristy needed two hands up, and a hoist to boot, but somehow she managed to clamber in before she collapsed on the seat. "Whew!" she breathed as the truck lurched forward. "I can't thank you enough!"

"Thanks for nothing," said the truck driver with a grin. He had gentle eyes and now spoke with typical Irish politeness. "It's a pleasure, miss. But what has you so upset on this fine morning? Isn't it a bit early to be off on a bicycle trip?"

Kristy nodded. "I promised to explain," she said, deciding that the man seemed trustworthy, "but it's going to sound silly. We just captured a poacher, my friend and I."

"Did you now?" The driver spoke indulgently, as though he were humoring a fanciful child. "And where have you got him if I may ask?"

"Tied to a tree near Mrs. Quinn's farmhouse," replied Kristy matter-of-factly. "The reason I'm in such a hurry is because we've got to get the guards."

The truck driver speeded up, although quite obviously he thought this American girl was daft. In less than five minutes he was turning in at the castle gate.

"You can drop me off here," Kristy suggested, but the man insisted on taking her all the way up the drive to where a pair of *gardai* cars were pulled up beside the vehicles the Henderson families had hired.

"Well," said the truck driver soothingly, "if it's the *gardai* you're after, miss, here they are in full force. You can tell them your story as quick as can be. What do you think of that?"

With every word the man spoke he was lowering the age to which he had ascribed her, until Kristy felt that she had acquired a level of intelligence in his eyes that about equaled Ned's. At another time she might have been amused, but today anxiety made her do no more than thank him quickly as he helped her unload Nora's bicycle. He backed the truck around and drove away as though his duty weren't quite done, but Kristy scarcely took time to wave good-bye.

Bursting into the castle hall without a thought for her muddy boots, Kristy found Sergeant Walsh and two strange young *gardai* talking to her father. "Daddy!" she cried, interrupting. "We've caught a poacher! It's Liam McMurrough, and we've got him tied to a tree down near Mrs. Quinn's farmhouse. Oh, hurry please, all of you! He might get loose, and Michael's there alone!"

234

16

By eleven o'clock that morning the castle drawing room
was filled with rows of dining-room chairs, which had
been added to the usual complement of furniture by Nora
and Mary, aided by Sergeant Walsh. It was beneath Superintendent Kelly to lend a hand, but he stood by and
nodded approvingly as the family filed in and took their
seats just as the clock struck the hour.

Grandma came first, her head high, her expression
indicating that she continued to find this whole affair
insupportable. "I sincerely hope this will wind things up,"
she said to anyone and everyone as she took a seat in one
of the three armchairs available.

"I'm sure it will, dear." Grandpa spoke soothingly, let
himself down to a straight chair beside her, and started
to pat her hand.

Kristy's parents, with Sam in tow, came in and ranged themselves on the sofa, which had been pushed back into the window embrasure to make more room. Kristy and Michael circled them and sat on the window sill, while Aunt Irene and Uncle Robert took seats in front of the grandparents. Ned burst from Mary's clutches and climbed on his mother's lap, then climbed down again when Mrs. O'Malley entered the room. "Where's Breeda?" he asked.

The rosy-faced woman smiled down at him. "Breeda's at our house, with Rosaleen and the rest. You can come play with her later. All right?"

"All right," Ned agreed and went back to his mother, while Mary took a seat beside Nora and Mrs. Quinn.

Liam McMurrough and the red-bearded man Kristy had glimpsed at the tower window were brought in last by the two *gardai*. McMurrough looked surly and the captive from the tower seemed sleepy and cowed.

"Where's Patrick O'Malley?" asked the superintendent, his eyes lighting on the absent man's wife.

"He's gone back to Cork this very morning," Mrs. O'Malley said cheerfully. "And sorry he'll be to miss the show."

Aunt Irene chuckled softly. However, Superintendent Kelly looked stern. In his opinion, this was no time for levity.

Portentously, he cleared his throat. Kristy was certain

that had there been a gavel handy he would have rapped for order. Then, in an appropriately formal manner, he reviewed the strange circumstances surrounding Fergus O'Malley's death. The succession of facts was known to everyone in the room, either directly or by hearsay. Not until the superintendent began to investigate the more recent developments did Kristy's interest revive.

"Mrs. Quinn, are you a relative of Liam McMurrough's?"

"Not a blood relative, sir. I'm his godmother," said the cook, substantiating Michael's information from his aunt.

"I understand that while Fergus O'Malley was alive McMurrough spent some time here at the castle?"

"A month at most," replied Mrs. Quinn, "and it wasn't the castle proper. Fergus just let him sleep in the tower."

"What month was that?"

"November, mainly. Liam left the end of the first week in December, when we started getting the place ready to let."

"Then where did McMurrough go?"

"I don't know," said Mrs. Quinn without hesitation. "I presume he went back to Fermoy."

Ned was becoming increasingly restless. "Excuse me, Superintendent," said his mother, "but if you have no questions you need to ask the children, I wonder if

Sam might be allowed to take Ned down to play with the young O'Malleys? With Mrs. O'Malley's permission, of course."

"I don't want to," said Sam.

"Sam, hop to it," his father ordered.

"Perhaps, ma'am," suggested Mary helpfully, "it would be best if I went along too."

The superintendent looked at Mary thoughtfully. "All right," he finally agreed with an ill-suppressed sigh, then went back to questioning Mrs. Quinn.

"Would it surprise you to know that your godson has been camping out at the property you own near Coolmucky Wood?"

"It would indeed!" said Mrs. Quinn promptly. "The place is little more than a ruin." She turned to McMurrough. "Is it true, Liam, that you've been using the farmhouse?"

Liam shrugged. "I was running a little short, and I couldn't see as you'd mind."

Mrs. Quinn didn't answer, but she looked as though she minded very much. Her mouth, usually soft and smiling, narrowed to a grim line, and she sat a little straighter in her chair.

"As a matter of fact, I'm afraid your farm has become a poacher's hangout," Superintendent Kelly continued, still addressing the cook. "Not only McMurrough, but Seamus O'Rourke, here, has been seen going and coming from there."

Kristy craned forward for a better look at the fellow who had been captured in the tower. So this was Seamus O'Rourke, who had been involved with Fergus and Liam in the fight at the Fermoy pub. He looked embarrassed and sheepish, but not really debased, and she wondered what part he had played in this scandalous business. Was he a poacher too?

"O'Rourke, you're accused of breaking and entering. What was your errand to the tower last night?" The superintendent's manner was brusque.

Dodging the question, Seamus said, "Not breaking, sir. You can't pin that one on me. I had a key."

"Why did you come there, O'Rourke?"

"Liam sent me. To get something he'd left behind."

"Something? What was it?"

Seamus wriggled in his seat and seemed to grow smaller. He glanced at Liam from the corner of his eye, as though he needed prompting, and finally muttered, "A jar of medicine."

"What kind of medicine?"

"How should I know?"

"Because I submit that what you were really looking for was a can of poison, in fact the very can that we took to headquarters in Cork. It's my duty to inform you that traces of the same poison were found in Fergus O'Malley's bloodstream."

Seamus suddenly looked frightened. He glanced at Liam again, desperately, but didn't speak.

239

"Furthermore, this isn't the first time you visited the tower," continued Superintendent Kelly briskly. "You were also searching for the poison sometime around three o'clock on Christmas morning. Isn't that right?"

Seamus leaped to his feet. "I never!" he cried, and turned to Liam accusingly.

McMurrough grinned sardonically. "So I stopped by Christmas eve, but it was Seamus who knew what the can looked like. I never seen it myself."

O'Rourke sank back into his chair, unwilling to dispute this statement. "It was never intended to poison poor Fergus," he said in a quavering voice that sounded sincere to Kristy. "It was just intended for the fish."

At Superintendent Kelly's prompting, Seamus poured out the whole story. He had learned of an insect poison, parathion, from a friend of his who worked in a greenhouse on a big estate near Castletownroche. This friend claimed that a smidgeon of the stuff could cause temporary paralysis, but that it wasn't lethal, and Seamus happened to tell Fergus about it one night at a Ballyhooly pub.

"What made you talk to Fergus about it?" asked Superintendent Kelly. "Why should it interest him?"

"He was a gardener, wasn't he? And there's a greenhouse here. I was just passing the time, that's all."

"Go on," said the superintendent.

"Well, Fergus asked if I could get him a wee bit of the

stuff. There were some experiments he'd like to make. I never thought of the salmon then, and that's the God's truth, though I did know Fergus and Liam were not above poaching with a few bags of spurge."

McMurrough snarled, "Keep your trap shut," but by now Seamus was apparently intent on saving his own skin and didn't care how much he incriminated Fergus O'Malley's accomplice.

"Anyway, I spoke to my friend and he packed an ounce or two of this white powder into a small can and pasted a label on it saying POISON."

"This can here?"

"Could be."

"When did you deliver it to O'Malley?" asked the superintendent.

"Let's see now. It must have been late November or early December. Anyway, it was the night Fergus and Liam got into the fight."

McMurrough reached up and touched the scar on his face as though he were remembering the incident bitterly. "This time we met at a pub in Fermoy," Seamus continued. "Liam was bent on dividing the poison in half, even though they were partners. He was afraid Fergus would steal a march on him and make off with a really big catch, because he'd been losing money to the bookies and needed a new stake pretty bad. Fergus was bound and determined he must test the effects of the stuff before

241

he'd dare dump any in the water. As I told you, he didn't want to kill the fish, you see, just stun them. First there was an argument. Then they came to blows. Some in the pub thought I was the cause of it all, and in a way I guess I was."

Seamus paused and scratched his head thoughtfully, while Grandpa glared at nobody in particular. It was obvious to Kristy that he was thinking of the plight of the poor salmon, and that he didn't have a shred of sympathy for these thieves.

"Be that as it may, when the fracas was over Liam landed in the hospital and Fergus made off with the poison, paying me little mind when I tried to tell him how dangerous it was. And I swear that's the last I saw of the can, from that day to this."

Michael leaned close to Kristy and whispered, "Do you believe him?"

Kristy hesitated to commit herself. "It sounds reasonable."

"How soon after the quarrel did you move out of the tower, McMurrough?" asked the superintendent.

"The very next day," claimed Liam promptly. "You can ask Nora if that's not the God's honest truth."

"It's the truth all right," said Nora, "and I, for one, was glad to be seeing the last of him." She glanced at Mrs. Quinn apologetically.

"Fergus had no right to let him stay here in the first

242

place," said Mrs. O'Malley, backing Nora up. "We all knew that."

The investigation continued, with Liam now the culprit being questioned. There was no point to denying he had been O'Malley's partner in crime, since he had been caught poaching this very morning, but McMurrough continued to insist that he had never touched the poison, nor had he indeed seen the can since that night at the Fermoy pub.

"Then what made you so anxious to find it, if not to destroy the evidence that you poisoned your partner?" The question was so completely unexpected that everyone in the room stirred and tried to get a glimpse of McMurrough's face.

"Me? Me poison Fergus? What for?"

"You'd had a falling out, hadn't you?"

"Sure, but I bore him no ill will," replied Liam. "We'd patched things up again before he died."

"That's *your* story. What proof have you?" asked the superintendent quickly.

Liam hesitated, apparently considering alternatives. He must either stand accused of O'Malley's murder or offer some pretty convincing evidence that he and his former confederate had ended up on good terms. "O.K.," he said, "you know about the spurge anyway. So I cut the stuff up in the hills, packed it in bags, and brought it down by muleback. Fergus ferried it across the river and stashed

243

it away in the graveyard, where the tinker picked it up yesterday afternoon. In other words, we were in business together again, long before Christmas. Why would I want to kill my partner? It doesn't make sense."

It didn't make sense to Kristy either, or to Michael. They glanced at each other in mute agreement. Liam had confessed to a career of poaching with Fergus in order to save himself from a far more serious rap.

At the back of the room, Grandpa could contain himself no longer. "That fellow should be in jail," he sputtered, "and all other poachers like him! The only way to preserve the salmon rivers of Ireland is to enforce the law!"

Spontaneously, Kristy's father and Uncle Robert applauded, although they were promptly silenced by the superintendent, who looked as though he would never understand the frivolity of the Americans. "Suppose you give us *your* version of Fergus O'Malley's death," he said to Liam caustically.

"That's easy. He committed suicide."

"Suicide?"

"Not on purpose, of course, but in a way of speaking. You already know he was testing out the strength of the poison. He knew it was potent, but he had high hopes for it, compared with spurge, which is bulky and hard to handle. Let me tell you, it's no fun to tread a sackful of that weed in the water on a cold winter day!"

244

"Did he realize it was an organic phosphate?" asked Superintendent Kelly.

"A what?"

"An organic phosphate, the first to be made available commercially, and never sold to amateur gardeners because of the danger to human life. Did he know that the slightest carelessness might result in serious injury or death?"

"I guess not," Liam muttered, and glanced at Seamus. "Did you know that?" he asked accusingly.

"The grower I got it from told me it was dangerous and I tried to tell you—the both of you—but you were too sore to listen. None of it's my fault."

The superintendent raised an eyebrow at this assertion, but he let it pass and returned his attention to McMurrough. "Exactly what kind of experiments were being conducted?" he asked.

"That I don't know, because Fergus wouldn't say. From the beginning he balked at telling me what he was up to, and it's my opinion he planned never to cut me in, but to go it alone." McMurrough hesitated. "I was pretty hot under the collar about the whole deal. Even before Fergus died I was hankering to get my hands on the poison and do a little experimenting myself."

"So you were searching for it in the tower Christmas eve?"

"Yeah," Liam admitted.

"How did *you* get a key?"

"That was easy. I made a wax impression of the old one and had a duplicate made. Later I loaned it to Seamus."

"I offered to help search for it, but only so I could get rid of the plagued poison," Seamus broke in, defensively.

"Why did you think O'Malley had hidden the poison in the tower?" Superintendent Kelly asked, ignoring the interruption and still addressing himself to McMurrough.

Liam shrugged. "It had to be somewhere. I'd already tried the boathouse, the night before." (That explains the light in the shrubbery and the broken padlock, Kristy thought to herself.) "I'd sure like to know where the poison did turn up, finally."

"In the salmon smokehouse," the superintendent replied. "And it may interest all of you to hear that only a few spoonfuls remained in the can. However, my men found a dusting of the powder on the ground under the central chimney where Fergus was in the habit of burning trash. From the pattern it made it's not hard to deduce that Fergus dropped the opened can and that some of the powder flew up in his face."

"Then he must have closed the can again and made his way out into the fresh air," put in Uncle Robert. "When I came across it, the lid was on tight."

Superintendent Kelly nodded. "Yes, we think he closed it and planned to destroy it, but by then he had taken a gasp of the stuff. In fact, he'd breathed in too much."

246

"You mean that could kill him?" Kristy burst out.

"Without a doubt," put in Kristy's father unexpectedly. "Parathion is so potent that it was removed from the market in the United States some time ago. You inhale it, or get enough on your hands, and you're in real danger."

The superintendent nodded. "In the case of Fergus O'Malley that danger ended in death."

"Then parathion wouldn't have done for poaching after all? It would have poisoned the fish, just as it poisoned Fergus," Kristy said.

"Right." Superintendent Kelly glanced around the room. "Now, are there any other questions?"

"Why the graveyard?" Kristy asked. "Why would he have headed for the graveyard?"

The officer shook his head. "We'll never know, but I could make an educated guess that he was about to move the spurge over to the gypsy camp. He must have stumbled against a gravestone on the way and cracked his head."

"I'd like to know how O'Malley got you interested in using spurge," Michael said, addressing Liam. "I thought that went out of style among poachers years ago."

Liam shrugged. "Fergus was always a great salesman. He showed me this story he'd found in a book telling about the big catches they made with spurge in the old days. I've never been able to resist a get-rich-quick scheme

247

and he knew it, but then when Seamus brought parathion into the picture, things got fouled up."

"Both Michael and I are interested in the preservation of the salmon, Superintendent," said Grandpa from his corner chair. "Can you tell us if there are other forms of poaching going on along the Blackwater?"

"There are a few fellows still taking fish with spiked poles, like the one McMurrough was using to spear the drugged fish, and there was a bit of illegal netting last season, but we've managed to clean that up."

"So you'd say the last of the big poachers has now been caught?" Michael asked, glancing at Liam, who looked increasingly surly.

"I'd say that, yes. Why do you ask?" The superintendent looked puzzled.

"Because I understand that Mr. Tompkins has agreed to stop dumping industrial waste from his sugarbeet factory if the *gardai* can stop the poaching. Maybe this is the time to see if he's as good as his word."

"I'll go call on him myself," promised the superintendent with a glint of anticipation in his eye, "and I thank you for the suggestion, young man!"

At this the matter stood. Without more ado Superintendent Kelly ordered the two *gardai* to take the culprits to the stationhouse to be booked, McMurrough on the charge of poaching and O'Rourke on the charge of illegal entry.

To Robert Russell he had the courtesy to apologize. "I'm truly sorry for what happened, sir," he said, "but you must admit the look of things was against you. As soon as I get back to Cork the charges will be vacated. I'm regretful, and I hope you have a pleasant holiday, in what time there is left."

He then shook hands all around, lingering when he came to Kristy and Michael. "We have a lot to thank you for," he said, then glanced at Michael's swollen jaw. "I hope you weren't too badly hurt."

"Of course he was hurt," said Grandma crisply, "as we all have been, in one way or another. Now I'll say good-day to you, Superintendent, and I trust you will not find it necessary to call on us again." The twinkle in her eyes belied the severity of Grandma's manner. As soon as the officer left the room, followed by Nora and Mrs. O'Malley, she gave a happy little chuckle and began making plans. "On New Year's day," she said with a sprightly air, "I think we should have a children's party and ask all the young O'Malleys to come to the castle at three o'clock in the afternoon. We'll make it a surprise for Ned. Mrs. Quinn, do you think you could make us some cookies?"

"Cookies, ma'am?"

"I keep forgetting that you call them biscuits. Biscuits and perhaps a cake?"

"A chocolate cake?"

"That would be lovely," said Grandma. "And Kristy,

do you think you could find some favors in Fermoy? Paper whistles or something of the sort?"

"That's my dear wife," said Grandpa with a grin. "Organizer Number One."

"Don't tease her, Grandpa!" Kristy crossed the room to slip her arm through his. "Grandma isn't like Aunt Irene and me. She doesn't like whodunits, either in books or in real life."

This remark led Aunt Irene to say, "There's one thing about *reading* a mystery, instead of living one. At the end you always get the various threads caught together and tied up."

"What's troubling you, Irene?" Kristy's mother asked.

"Well, for one thing, what's going to happen to the gypsies? They're guilty of transporting the spurge Liam used, aren't they?"

Her husband shrugged. "I rather doubt if that could be counted a misdemeanor—hauling a load of weeds."

"I concur," said Kristy's father, rocking back and forth on his heels before the fire. "They may have been perfectly innocent, and even if they weren't, I doubt that the guards will try to catch up with them. In times of trouble the gypsies, like old soldiers, seem to just fade away."

Grandma clapped her hands. "No more talk about any of this!" she commanded.

"Haven't I heard that before?" her son asked teasingly.

Uncle Robert turned to his niece. "After lunch," he

suggested, "I'll drive you to Fermoy to hunt for party favors. We can tie Michael's bike to the back of the car and drop him off on the way."

In town, Michael stayed with Kristy until the last possible moment, because he was catching the train for Dublin in the morning. He braved the curious stares of clerks, who were too polite to ask him how he had hurt his face, and followed her from store to store until she had found the things she sought.

Uncle Robert, meanwhile, had errands of his own. He wanted to buy such assorted items as toothpaste, cheese and crackers, yogurt for Ned, and color film for himself. "I'm planning to go out on the river with Steve as soon as the salmon season opens," he said, "to get some action shots."

Kristy and Michael, after half an hour of shopping, carrying big, flimsy paper bags full of small purchases, strolled back to the car along the twilit street. Lights gleamed dimly behind cloudy panes, trucks rattled by, and women in dark coats scurried along the sidewalks like plump gray mice.

"I wish I didn't have to leave," Michael said.

"I do too."

"Have I told you," Michael asked as he looked down at Kristy lingeringly, "that you're a very brave girl?"

"I—brave?" Kristy shook her head so vigorously that her long hair swung back and forth across her shoulders.

251

"You're the one with courage. Why, this morning, down by the river, I was scared half to death!"

"You certainly didn't show it," said Michael proudly. "I never saw such spunk! My cheek is nothing compared to the egg you managed to raise on Liam's head."

"No more compliments. You'll spoil me." Kristy raised a forefinger and placed it gently against Michael's lips.

To her surprise, he caught her hand and kissed it lightly. "You don't know how I'll miss you," he said. "I'll be counting the days."

"Don't worry. I'll be there when school starts. You know," Kristy added pensively, "now that all the excitement is over here, I'm actually anxious to get back to school!"

This was the nearest she dared come to telling Michael how much she liked him. To be sure he understood, she looked up at his face shyly, just as Uncle Robert accosted them.

"Hey, you kids!" he cried. "You walked right past the car."

Then, as he helped untie Michael's bicycle from the rear of the little Irish Ford, he remembered an errand he'd forgotten. As though they had been handed a reprieve, Kristy and Michael leaned against the fender, talking in whispers, until they saw him hurrying back across the street.

"It seems to me I just got to Fermoy yesterday!" Michael complained as parting became inevitable. "Where has the time gone?"

"I'll tell you where it's gone," replied Kristy with a smile. "It has gone to a very good cause! And all the fishermen who love the Blackwater should be grateful. Let's hope the ghost of Ballyhooly will never walk again!"

About the Author

Betty Cavanna grew up in Haddonfield, New Jersey, and was gradua-
ted from Douglass College, where she majored in journalism. It was
during her work for Westminster Press in Philadelphia that she
became interested in writing stories herself, and in 1943 she became
a full-time writer of books for young people. She holds an honorary
membership in Phi Beta Kappa for her outstanding contribution to
the field of juvenile literature. In private life Miss Cavanna is Mrs.
George Russell Harrison. She and her husband live in Concord,
Massachusetts.